The Urbana Free Library

To renew: call 217-367-4057
or go to "*urbanafreelibrary.org*"
and select "Renew/Request Items"

		DATE DUE	5-13

Starlite Terrace

THE GERMAN LIST

PATRICK ROTH

Starlite Terrace

TRANSLATED BY KRISHNA WINSTON

LONDON NEW YORK CALCUTTA

GOETHE-INSTITUT

This publication was supported by
a grant from the Goethe-Institut India

Seagull Books, 2012

First Published in German as *Starlite Terrace*
© Suhrkamp Verlag, Frankfurt am Main, 2004

English translation © Krishna Winston, 2012

ISBN-13   978 0 8574 2 082 4

British Library Cataloguing-in-Publication Data
A catalogue record for this book is available from the British Library.

Typeset in Dolly-Roman by Seagull Books, Calcutta, India
Printed and bound by Hyam Enterprises, Calcutta, India

And in the end you wind up dying
all alone on some dirty street. For what?
For nothing. For a tin star.

> Lon Chaney Jr. to Gary Cooper in *High Noon*

Intellige te alium mundum esse in parvo
et esse intra te Solem, esse Lunam, esse etiam
stellas.

Understand that you are a second world
in a microcosm, and that in you are the sun,
the moon, and also the stars.

> Origen, Homiliae on *Leviticus* 5.2

Every man's condition is a solution in
hieroglyphic to those inquiries he would
put. He acts it as life, before he apprehends
it as truth.

> Ralph Waldo Emerson, *Nature*

CONTENTS

Starlite Terrace

ONE

The Man at Noah's Window

A while ago—it had been pouring for days and we were sitting in Noah's Deli on Ventura Boulevard, by now almost flooded—Rex, who always ate his breakfast by the window, told us that his father had been an excellent step dancer but a veritable magician with his hands. In the fifties, it seemed, he had been hired now and then for hand close-ups.

'So in a Western—' Rex said, 'in those days the studios were making tons of Westerns, both for the movies and for television—when they wanted to shoot a card trick or gun play in close-up, my father was sometimes hired and would then supposedly do the hand stunts for the star.'

'Supposedly?' I asked, thinking to myself, well, did he or didn't he have a hand in Westerns?

Rex said that when his father was buried in Forest Lawn Cemetery, an extra told him that his father had been hired for several close-ups of Gary Cooper's hands in *High Noon*. Probably for the shoot-out at the end.

'Yet another legend,' Pete commented sarcastically, 'that "Rex Judaeorum" wants us to believe.' Pete enjoyed bickering with Rex. These disputes helped the two oldsters get their circulation going. They both lived in my apartment complex, Starlite Terrace, and met up every morning at Noah's for this companionable sparring.

'Rex Judaeorum', King of the Jews—that was the envious nickname Pete had started using for his age-mate once he noticed the special dispensation Rex enjoyed at the Jewish deli, which Rex had patronized since it opened. Rex did not have to stop to pay Jaffa, the cashier, for his first bagel with cream cheese and lox. He had quickly won the heart of Luz, Jaffa's recently hired helper from El Salvador, who spread butter on bagels behind the counter and waited on the customers. Rex not only guessed Luz's middle name on the first try but also came up with that of her son, and from then on he never forgot to ask the young mother how her *niño* was doing, usually as she was performing the delicate operation of spearing strips of lox with a fork and transferring them to freshly toasted split bagels.

It was a little past seven, and as yet we were the only patrons at Noah's. From Pete's hot coffee a mild hazelnut aroma wafted over our table by the window. He had filled a paper cup with Chelsea Blend from the thermos dispenser at the coffee bar. This flavor always inspired nostalgia, reminding us of Clinton, his daughter, and his time in office.

'Watch it, Rex!' Pete commented, 'Watch it when you speak of the One and Only Great One!' Gary Cooper had large, beautiful hands, he said, not hands that could easily be replaced by someone else's. He, Pete, had seen the film in the uncut version, before its release. He certainly could not recall any 'substitute hands'. 'Maybe it was some other film, some other Western,' Pete said, 'in which your father supposedly served as a hand double.'

'No, supposedly it was *High Noon*,' Rex insisted.

'What does "supposedly" mean?' I asked again.

'Well, that's what I heard. My father died in '53, a few months after they finished shooting the film.'

Pete refused to let go. 'Wait a minute. In *High Noon*, Gary Cooper is no whiz with a revolver. It's all he can do to keep the killers at bay. Why would they have needed a hand double? What revolver magic? Someone was pulling your leg.'

'Not necessarily,' I defended Rex. 'Maybe certain shots were at least planned, or were shot just in case. Or his father substituted for one of the other actors in *High Noon*, who knows?'

'No, no, it was Cooper,' Rex insisted proudly. 'It was for Cooper.'

That extra had veritably raved about his father. According to him, Rex's father had always made a point of shaking hands with the actors whose hands were to be represented by his. In this case, he had offered his hand to Gary Cooper and held the actor's longer than usual, memorizing the form and special properties of the other man's hand. Supposedly that enabled him later to make his hand as good as identical to the actor's in close-ups.

'He had big hands,' Rex commented. 'Big hands and, I assume, good-looking ones. Obviously. Otherwise he wouldn't have gotten those close-up jobs.'

'Which is precisely what I'm calling into question, and not only that,' Pete countered. 'At the time, see, I . . .'

'Big deal,' Rex interrupted him, 'Even if you'd been the greatest pistol virtuoso west of the Pecos, a close-up of your hands would have destroyed the impression. People would have forgotten all about your skill with the pistol as they stared in amazement at your stumpy little fingers. "Pete's little freak show" is what it would have been, not a close-up of hands firing and reloading in a flash.'

'Seriously now,' Pete responded, 'I remember you told me once that your father regularly beat your mother. With those big, beautiful hands.'

Rex stared out into the rain in silence. As if the longer he stared out the window at the strings of rain, the more effectively they bound together his father's contradictory hands, cleansing them, so to speak. Suddenly he turned to me—as if I had asked him a question and it were his duty to set me straight.

'It's true, I hardly remember my parents. About twenty years ago, someone showed me a couple of old photos, allegedly of them. Strangers. I wouldn't have recognized them. When I think about them, I don't see faces. It's also true that I more or less clung to them. I mean, I hung on to my mother's skirt or apron when they fought, and was swung back and forth. They never hit me, at least not that I recall, but I hung on and was swung back and forth pretty hard by their blows and violent movements. That I remember. Also that we were living in a trailer at the time. There was an area between the stove and the sink, somewhat wider than the rest of the trailer, and that was where he hit her when they'd been drinking.'

Rex hesitated, as if he could not rid his mind of that image so easily.

'My father disappeared when I'd just turned six. It was my first day of school and he'd gone with me as far as the entrance. We were late and the lawn in front of the school was deserted—not another child in sight. We stood by the steps and I remember that the top step was level with my head. I stood on tiptoe and peered down a dark hallway and into a class-room. The children were sitting quietly at their desks. A teacher was walking up and down the rows. Fear seized hold of me and I turned to my father. But he was gone, had almost reached the next corner. I waved, thinking I'd run after him, as if I'd forgotten something. But he didn't see me. So I seized the opportunity and ran in the opposite direction, to one of the vacant lots where we kids sometimes played. I squatted down and lit a cigarette to calm my nerves. Several days passed before the teacher came to see us and my mother learned that I'd been skipping school since the first day. I crouched behind the trailer, out-side under the kitchen window, and eavesdropped. At first I could hardly make out anything. Then I heard my mother crying, as she loudly contradicted the teacher: "No, he won't be coming back." It sounded as though she was determined to shield me from the most terrible danger, from school and teachers. I felt so grateful to her that I'd have liked to pop up by the window and cry with her. But then

I realized who she meant; it was my father who wouldn't be back. It's funny: he ran away the same day as me.'

'You never saw him again?' I asked.

Rex shook his head.

'During the Second World War,' he said, 'there was a play on Broadway that everyone was talking about. *Life with Father*. A huge hit. At the end, after the third act, the audience always remained seated. Until someone came out from behind the curtain and said, "That's all, that's it, that's all there is." The audience wanted life with father to go on. The fathers were all away in the war, see.'

Pete, who had seen the movie but not the play, made some comment—I no longer recall what.

When Rex quoted those words spoken by the man from behind the curtain—'That's all, that's it, that's all there is'—in my mind's eye, I saw the curtain billow, saw the folds briefly bunch up—that was the trigger—and was unexpectedly overcome by the memory of a dream from the night before.

In the dream, I was sitting with Rex by the window at Noah's, just as I was doing now. Rex had his back to the wall and had put his feet up on another chair. He was talking with someone on a cell phone, although in reality he did not own one. In my dream,

I concluded that Rex was preoccupied and had no idea what was about to happen right outside our window. Troubled, I stood up and looked out onto Ventura Boulevard. The street lay there in the midday light, which was pale as it sometimes is before a storm, and swept bare, like the street in *High Noon*. In my dream it did not occur to me, however, that the street was deserted. Less than a hundred paces from Noah's, to the west, in front of the Bank of America building and Border's Books, something was brewing. Dark cloud formations that had come down to street level were in motion, hovering at first, until a thrashing wind from the north began to drive them around in a circle, and they rotated faster, then uncontrollably fast, gushing in a foamy stream, swirling into a tight ball, rearing up to form a head, flaming in grays and purples, as if fire were darting through them. 'Man, it's moving too fast out there . . . take a look!' I shouted at Rex. But he continued talking on his phone as if he did not hear me. I looked out the window and knew I would not make it home. Any minute now, all hell would break loose. I saw that the wind gusts were rounding up clouds from all directions, bringing them together too fast, and now threatening to let loose with terrible force. I ran to shut Noah's door, that much I recall. Then I ducked into the wall across from Rex. That is to say, in the dream there was no wall but instead a dark, window-less space into which I fled as everything began to shudder and shake. I called to Rex, who was still on the phone and did not hear me. At the last moment, I threw myself to the ground, clasping my hands over my head to protect it, as panes of glass and the doorframe rattled, the storm from the boulevard descended with a howl and raged along Noah's, smashing its glass facade and ripping it out of its moorings.

At this point in the dream, as at this point in my memory of it, I woke up. *Berserk.* The word came to me while my eyes were still closed. The image had gone dark, darkened by the berserk power of the storm itself. But then, out of the darkened image, emerged the echo of something different, something entirely different, that rang out briefly, brightly—and in my nostrils was an animal smell, in my ears the sound of hoofs. But I could not hold on to this image, and although I tried to follow it, my eyes wide open, it vanished.

I found it oddly unsettling that the scene here in the deli resembled my dream in its general outlines. For besides Rex and me, only Pete was there in Noah's. Without our noticing, Luz had probably gone back into the baking area and Jaffa had not yet put in an appearance that morning. Rex seemed distracted, as in my dream. He was preoccupied with something and was bickering with Pete again. I looked out onto the boulevard towards the west. True, there were no wind-whipped clouds massing at street level but the illuminated Bank of America building and the neon tubes framing Border's dissolved in the ceaseless ropes of rain, which frayed into strands as the wind drove them against the window.

Abruptly, Pete stood up and reached for his umbrella.

'I've had enough of your insults,' I heard him say. And as he walked past me: 'This guy wants to turn me into his keeper!'

Confused, I got up and tried to hold Pete back. 'What's the matter now?' I asked. Instinctively, I wanted to avoid being left alone with Rex—as in my dream.

'Rex Judaeorum,' Pete commented spitefully. And then to Rex: 'You're the one who's a coward.'

Pete shook off my hand, refusing to let me stop him.

'By the way, you'll be next,' he said, and opened his umbrella, which the wind threatened to carry off the moment he stepped outside.

I had remained standing by the wall closest to the door, the wall that in my dream had not existed.

Countless times I had passed the three old framed black-and-white photos that hung there without paying much attention to them. Now, as the dream still held me in thrall, it occurred to me that they might offer clues to what the wall concealed, to the dark space that in my dream had offered me protection. As if the wall were merely heavy fabric stretched over a frame. If I succeeded in reading these pictures I had previously ignored, the wall would be transformed into a window, providing a glimpse into the world hidden behind the screen.

The photo in the middle was the size of a large poster. It showed a crowded Jewish street market around the turn of the century, photographed from the roof of a house in New York's Greenwich Village. Several children running in the gutter past the market stalls had been captured by the photographer only in a blur, but the rest of the crowd, carefully evaluating the many wares and deciding what to buy, could be seen in sharp focus. My eye fell, seemingly by chance, on a boy who was unhitching a horse amid the stream of humanity, starting to pull the animal away from a darkly laden cart. His forearm was blurred up to the elbow from the rapid movement towards the bridle, giving the impression that at any moment the horse would trot away, led by the boy. In fact, I caught myself waiting for the clang of hooves on the cobblestones.

The smaller photo on the left showed a portly woman wrapped in shawls and seated majestically in an easy chair, guarding the entrance to an empty shop. On the shop window, behind which the display had been cleared out, someone had painted, in large white letters that had started to run, FISH WOMAN MOVED TO MONTANA. The third photo hung next to Noah's mezuzah, the finger-length wooden capsule that held, like an ark, the word commanding love for the One God. Some of the faithful kissed their fingertips before touching it upon entering and leaving. The photo showed Einstein with Ben-Gurion, the image no larger than a hand mirror.

But how was one supposed to read these photographs? Was it pointless to search them for clues, to intuit something in their reality that connected them with mine?

'So are you acting offended, too?' I heard Rex saying behind me.

'Oh, not at all.' I turned to look at him.

Rex was sitting there, his head leaning against the window, as if he could still see Pete, who had long since disappeared into the rain.

'What were the two of you quarreling about just now?'

'I had the gall,' Rex said, 'to cast doubt on Pete's memory and to quote June, who mentioned his

14

excesses involving alcohol and . . . well, never mind. I was fool enough to ask the man for a favor.'

'And?'

'He promptly chickened out.'

Rex looked at me. 'That's how it is,' he said, 'We're always preoccupied and don't want to see or hear what others need.'

He pointed to the photographs on the wall.

'No,' I said, 'I was only . . . those pictures reminded me of something. Last night, when . . .'

I wondered if I should tell Rex about my dream. I wanted to avoid describing the actual vision but I could not get it out of my mind. I said, as if the idea had come to me when I looked at the pictures, 'Did you see the pictures from Jerusalem yesterday? In the *L.A. Times*?'

'What pictures?' Rex asked. 'I didn't get around to reading the paper yesterday.'

'There were three photos . . . single images captured by some sort of surveillance camera, I think. In the first one you saw a ballroom filled with wedding guests, dancing. The bride and groom were being carried through the crowd on chairs by their friends. Somewhere on the fourth floor of a Jerusalem hotel. Suddenly the floor gave way . . .'

'Sounds like a nightmare,' Rex commented.

'Yes, a nightmare,' I said, and fell silent as the middle picture came back to me—the ballroom's floor was gone, except for a rim of rubble, and had taken the floors below down with it. The people who had been dancing and singing just seconds before were by now almost unrecognizable, dark splinters being sucked downward in a bright vortex that distorted the perspective to the point that I no longer knew what I was seeing. Distorted it as if I were not supposed to be able to imagine it. My memory fled to the next picture—a gaping hole from which dust welled up, and very near the camera, by the wall, the kneeling figure of a woman with an injured eye who was trying to feel where the abyss opened up.

Rex, too, was silent, as if following this nightmare in his mind, as if the images I was seeing had communicated themselves to him as he gazed out the window. As if the confused web being woven by the strands of rain pulled everyone capable of seeing from the first image to the second, from the second to the third, but then from that one to the final one, already present and lurking within us.

As if caught in the vortex myself, I was drawn into the total annihilation that had swept these people away in a matter of seconds, the annihilation that had been lying in wait for them under the floor. Something is lying in wait under the floor or behind the wall, I thought, reminded of the wall in Noah's by which I was still standing. The wall that had opened in my dream to save me.

In reality—a reality that once I had become aware of it appeared no less odd than my dream—in reality Noah's shared this wall with Hooper's Camera, the photo shop next door. A photo shop, of all things! I had gone there to get the passport photos I needed for the trip I was about to take. By the way, wasn't the name Hooper the same as Cooper? If you aspirate the c, already you are passing through the wall into the ...

'Strange, the things you remember,' Rex interrupted my thoughts. He gestured to me to join him by the window. 'Why you suddenly remember something. For instance, I just recalled something I realized in 1975, something I hadn't thought about in thirty-five years. Down that way—' he gestured towards the east, 'at the corner of Van Nuys, the light had just turned green and I crossed Ventura Boulevard to go to the newsstand. Nothing out of the ordinary. Suddenly, as I was walking, I remembered what my mother was. She was a hooker. It was in the town where I spent the first years of my life, Madera—you wouldn't know it. It's north of Fresno, in the San Joaquin Valley. Suddenly, I see these images before me, out of nowhere. I must have been five or six and

I was running towards what we used to call a motor court, a kind of motel. Someone had given me a quarter and I wanted to go to the movies. I always had some coins on me. I knew all kinds of smutty verses and songs and I'd get up on a table and perform. People would laugh themselves silly and often give me their small change. At any rate, I remembered running to one of the motel doors, turning the knob, pushing it open and—the door opened only a crack. The safety chain was on. I pressed my eye to the crack and—saw something. It looked like a dark blood spot on the floor by the bed. Next to it a tipped-over nail polish bottle. Then my mother's head on a pillow, and a man's face above her. I could make out his face easily, but hers ... all I saw was her nose and one eye as she arched her back to see me. "I want to go to the movies," I said. "So-and-so gave me money, can I?" And she said, "All right, but come right back when it's over." I closed the door and dashed to the movie theater. It's weird. The whole scene came back to me in a flash.'

'Where was your father at that time?'

'They were already separated by then, I guess. As I said, one day he simply took off. Sometimes she'd leave me with the waitresses she knew at a cafe. I still have a thing for waitresses, you know? They watched out for me, made sure I was OK. There was always something to eat, and I liked hanging out with them. In those days waitresses all smoked Pall Malls—as a kid I called them "Paul Mauls"—because they were longer than regular cigarettes, and mild. They came in a red pack, I remember. The waitress who happened to be watching me would say, "You watch this for me," would take one more puff and put her cigarette down on the ashtray next to the cash register. I'd pretend to keep my eye on the glowing tip for a while. Sometimes, I would get almost hypnotized, staring at the red smudge left by her lipstick. When the threads of smoke fanned out in a draft or wafted almost horizontally into the room and the good warm smell circled back to me, the woman's warmth and her mouth were right there, as if they had been missing me and had come back, disembodied, to be with me. The waitress would bring a customer his dinner or take an order and when she returned three or four minutes later, the Pall Mall was still lit and quite a bit of it was left. "You did a good job," she'd say. The women didn't realize that I'd already been smoking for ages.'

'They loved you.'

At first Rex seemed to be weighing my words. Then he remarked in a strange non sequitur, 'Besides, they were mild.'

He paused, tasting the cigarettes in his memory.

'One time when I was eight or nine,' he said finally, 'and still outdoors after dark, a patrol car pulled up beside me. The cops wanted to know what I was up to. "Where do you live, son?" In those days they still said "son" when they were dealing with a boy. They sounded kind. So, of course I gave them the address. But then they wanted to drive me home. "Hop in, sonny boy," they said. When we got to the house, they insisted on coming upstairs with me. I unlocked the door and somehow, maybe because I was embarrassed, I saw the room as if for the first time. Saw it through their eyes. It was a cramped, bare space, and in one corner lay a mattress, my bed, with a couple of my things on the floor. That was it. I swear, I'd never noticed before. Suddenly, with the two cops there, I wished there were more stuff in the room. Or . . . my mother. In an apron and holding a wooden spoon, you know. A roast in the oven. I think I even called out to her, because I was ashamed. The two cops were whispering to each other, and I trotted to the door and called out loudly. As if she had just stepped out for a moment to borrow milk or baking powder or such from a neighbor. But the policemen took me with them: "You're coming with us, son," and the next time I saw my mother was in court. Yes . . . I think that was the last time I saw her. Can that be? Was that really the last time?' Rex asked slowly, as if he were doing the math in his head, as if it might be possible . . . Then he continued, 'I was placed with a succession of families, each time in a different place. I could have been adopted but I never managed to make it through the trial period. That was a year. After two or three months, I always had to be transferred, sent somewhere else. One time they put me in a rich family. The man was called Vic Victor and he owned paint factories. Victory Paint— have you heard of it? "We sell the color of glory"— that was his slogan. He had a little daughter and they had the glorious idea of adopting a little brother for her. The Victors had my entire life planned out— which I didn't know at the time. I was supposed to study economics at USC, vote Republican and receive half the company as my inheritance. Every day the man gave me more schoolwork, more than I could ever handle. At some point, I must have gone crying to Mrs. Victor and I felt so awful that I asked her where I was going to be sent the next month. "Where?" she asked in amazement, "You're staying here, of course. We're going to adopt you." No more talk of a trial year. After that, I did everything I could to get them to dislike me. I made the little girl cry, claimed in her parents' presence that she'd done things she couldn't possibly have done, and so on. I paid for it when I got to the next family. I really thought they had it in for me, the ... Oppenheimers, that was their name. I was deposited with them around Easter and for the first few days, I ate well. But one evening, the bread they gave me was hard as rock. Flat and tasteless. Then I was supposed to eat from a platter where several foods were laid out. I took something—and almost choked on it. It was horseradish, I think. Mr. Oppenheimer burst out laughing when he saw my face getting redder and redder. And his wife pounded me on the back, while I gagged and gasped for air. No sooner had I calmed down than they told me that the fraction of a second when I couldn't breathe had been my death. That freaked me out. All right, now that I was alive again, they said, I'd been freed by that little choking death from all the bad stuff that had ever happened to me or that I had ever done. It was clear to me right away what they were referring to. I thought they were secretly out to avenge the Victors' little girl. The Oppenheimers must have sensed my suspicion. They explained to me that those foods had religious meaning and that this would go on for seven more days. That filled me with despair, and the next chance I got, I ran away. I was caught, but at some point there were no more families. After that, it was a succession of homes, the usual,' Rex said, as if I were familiar with the routine, as if everyone had the same experience.

'Unbelievable,' I said, 'that in all your wandering you never ran into your mother again. Or did you?' I asked, like someone who in fact never did have such experiences.

Rex did not answer.

'Didn't you even try?'

Maybe I hoped to hear him say, 'No, I hated my mother. I was glad to be rid of her.' But Rex remained calm and matter-of-fact, never uttering a bad word about her. As if he wanted me to understand that hunting down someone like her would have been pointless, he remarked, 'See, I never knew where she was. I was completely in the dark. For instance, I was born down in Long Beach. That's what's on my birth certificate. Why? I have no idea. Maybe my father was looking for work on the docks. But maybe not. Maybe she was visiting someone there. Later, she took a room near where soldiers were stationed and her services were in demand. Then, I don't know why, she must have come back to Madera at one point. I was eleven. Someone fetched me from the home I was in at the time and drove me to Madera. We stopped in front of a house by an intersection in the north end of town. I was taken upstairs to the second floor and dropped off in a cramped, overheated living room.

'Four or five older people were sitting around. One of them I recognized, a saddle-maker. He'd let me watch sometimes when he was cutting leather for saddles. When I saw him, I was reminded of the old Civil War veteran, his grandfather or father, who he called Nick and who always hung around the shop. In the winter, Nick wore a kind of shirt made of bearskin and sometimes, on national holidays, you could see him stalking along stiffly in the Madera parade, wearing his shabby gray uniform and without his cane. At eleven he'd joined the Confederates as a drummer boy. He was an orphan. He witnessed countless battles and one time had to hide inside his drum, the saddler told me. To me, in those days "eleven" was still "more than ten" and infinitely far off. But now I was eleven myself. The mood in the room was so crushing that I didn't dare tell him that I remembered him and the old man—and how he'd hid in the drum.

'I'd imagined that inside the drum it must have smelled of animal. That's the smell that surrounds me all day as I'm drumming on the taut animal hide, before I crawl inside at night, so no one can find me. It smelled of the death of the animal, a bear, I imagined, which kept me safely hidden under its bearskin shirt, spread its clothlike skin over me, held its death over me like a shield, to keep my death at bay all through the night.

24

'And that smell, it seemed to me, wafted into that cramped living room where we were sitting, as if the walls had let the soot of memory permeate them. I got up, took a few steps and was held back by the others. As if they'd noticed that I smelled something and wanted to keep me from tracking it down. Behind the door to the next room we'd heard sounds from time to time, a metallic clanging, a scraping and pulling, a rustling, drops falling, and later, cloth being torn into strips.

'I don't know when I realized that my mother— my mother's corpse—was lying in the next room. No one had said anything to me, or at least anything that would have made it clear to me why I was sitting here, why we'd gathered. I'd assumed it had something to do with me being transferred to another home. And since this was a private house, I thought with surprise that maybe they wanted to try putting me with a family again. Madera would have been OK by me. The longer we sat there, the more familiar the room seemed, though I was sure I'd never been there before. I must have recognized some objects she owned when we were still together.

'As I said, it was hot, very hot, and in such cases the funeral director came to the house and prepared the body there. The door to the next room opened and I saw a man in black standing on the threshold. He hesitated when he caught sight of me. Even though I didn't know him. It was embarrassing for him. We had to get up to let him through to the stairs—that was how cramped it was. He was carrying two heavy pails filled with liquid. In one bucket, it sloshed up to the rim, looking like dark nail polish. At that point someone pulled me over to the window . . . and opened it.'

Rex broke off his account. But he could see that I was waiting for him to continue. He lowered his eyes and ran the edge of his hand over the table, almost all the way to the window. Then, haltingly, as if it were a capsule, the visible container of the invisible, he touched the glass with his fingertips. Just briefly. I saw rain flowing around the fingerprints and the coldness of the glass obliterating the marks. Finally he went on:

'From this window, at the end of Yosemite Avenue, I could see the movie theater I'd gone to every day. Madera is the first town, the first dump I remember. Flat, dry, windy, a little like Texas. Long ago, during the Gold Rush, when they were clear-cutting in the Sierras, the logs were floated by canal down from the mountains—to Madera. That's Spanish for wood. When people asked me where I was from, all my life I said, "Madera. I'm from Madera." That sounded solid, as if I knew for sure where I belonged. It was in Madera she met my father. When she was buying shoes, by the way. He was a salesman in a shoe store located not even twenty feet from the movie house I could see from the window that had just been opened.'

It was as if Rex were looking through Noah's window at a second, invisible window behind it, a window that had always been waiting for him out there and now opened for him, under the pressure of the incessant rain.

'So it was over there, a few steps from the movie house, that it all began,' Rex said. 'I don't think I was aware of it at eleven. I held on to the windowsill as if the room might suddenly tip backward and hurl me through the open door into the back room with the corpse. Strange, I don't remember the burial. Maybe they didn't take me along. Towards evening, the man who'd brought me there drove me back to the home. Past the shoe store and the movie theater, into which people were crowding.'

'What was it called?'

He thought for a moment.

'The shoe store where they met was called . . . Bramer. Bramer's, that's it.'

'I mean the movie theater next door. Do you remember what it was called?'

He thought some more, then suddenly came up with the name and I could see he was quite incredulous at what he had stumbled on.

'You know what?' he said, 'It was the REX.' He laughed. 'I've no idea why that never occurred to me before.'

'You were named after the movie theater your parents always went to.'

He nodded and looked away, through the rain-streaked window pane, as if the evening showing were just starting across the way at the REX.

'And this is the first time you've realized that?' I asked. 'Today, just by chance, sixty years later?'

'If I say so, that's how it is,' he said. 'That's how it is. The REX was the movie theater my father always went to after work. And maybe he took my mother to the REX. Aaah . . . ,' said Rex, as if this realization had not only conjured up the magic he had experienced as a child at the movies but also given him power over his past. As if suddenly, instead of always seeing himself as an accident, as an abortion his mother hadn't succeeded in carrying out, he had been moved by this insight into the center or at least closer to the center.

Perhaps embarrassed at revealing how pleased he was to have discovered the source of his name, thereby also revealing himself as the eternal outsider, he changed the subject.

'Man, you have no idea what the movies were in those days. The movies in Madera. There were only two theaters. One of them was the MADERA, which was expensive, and the other, where a ticket cost only ten or fifteen cents, was the REX. The REX next door. Always packed, you know, total chaos. Often we stretched out on the stage because every seat was taken and stared straight up at the ratty screen. Westerns, gangster flicks, comedies, all B-movies. The program changed three times a week. And they always had double bills in those days. First came the cartoon, then the newsreel and finally the first feature. During the previews of coming events, especially when the hero clinched with the heroine or swooped in to kiss her or the bad guy went galloping out of town, we'd toss our empty popcorn boxes at the screen and then . . . we'd shut up. Shut up for the second feature. A four-hour ritual.'

He fell silent, animated yet contented, and it became clear to me that Rex could see his parents before him, this unknown couple whom, as he admitted, he would not have recognized in any photo or on the street. His imagination had inserted them among that wild horde of children occupying the REX, two people whispering to one another.

And what were they whispering about?

It was about his name, the name they would give him. While he was still in her belly, his name had long since captured their imagination and was whispering to them what he should be called. It came from the screen, that name did, through the ratty fabric, through the smoke from cannon salvos, waving pennants, whizzing arrows and lances, as a battle in black and white raged around the fortress; it zoomed over the rows of spectators, staring open-mouthed at the screen, wormed its way into his father's ear and from there to his mouth, and he leaned over to whisper to his mother the inspiration that had reached his tongue.

I thought I could see how this thought process had filled him with the secret strength he now felt. It seemed to Rex as if he had baptized himself REX. As if he, REX, had given himself a home and could take credit for his parents' best hours and for countless imaginary walks the two had taken after the movies. He, the prompter, the guide, REX, who had whispered from his screen to his parents, telling them what name they should give him. Long before he glimpsed the light of the world. While he was still the light of the world, every evening after work, in the light-dappled darkness of the REX. Three times a week—space, light and sound—prized and reasonably priced—the REX ritual.

'And it must have been in the REX,' I said, 'that your father saw Gary Cooper for the first time.'

'Yes, of course,' Rex said. 'Come to think of it, he saw Cooper in *Beau Geste*—that's the first film with Coop I remember—or *The Westerner* or *Mr. Deeds Goes to Town* or *The Lives of a Bengal Lancer* . . .'

'That was Hitler's favorite film, by the way,' I remarked.

'Really?'

I was irked at myself for having interrupted him.

'. . . or *The Adventures of Marco Polo*,' Rex continued, as if he had to smooth over the reference to Hitler. 'Or *The Pride of the Yankees*, one of those early Cooper films in the REX. And to think he was holding my mother's hand! Maybe a little tipsy but romantic; she must have liked that, in the movie theater, in the REX. He held her hand and didn't know, couldn't have guessed, that his hand would one day take the place of the hero's, in *High Noon*, and that those two hands were more or less identical, that of the hero up on the screen and the one down below resting on the dress of my mother, tipsy, pregnant and infatuated, in the REX.'

While he was speaking, filled with enthusiasm and hardly addressing himself to me anymore, he stared out the window into the rainy morning. It was as if he were painting a picture that he wanted to correct here and there. But at the mention of the film's title, I was suddenly reminded of the signature melody in *High Noon*.

I had seen the film in Germany when I was a child, not in '53 when it was first released there, but maybe in the late fifties. The images themselves could not be separated from that melody, the song that now came to mind. It hovered over the shots of the bleached sky, the bare-swept street which Marshal Kane, aka Gary Cooper, must walk down to confront the men who arrived on the noon train to kill him. Before that decisive moment, he is abandoned by the woman, Grace Kelly, the stunning woman in white, whom he married only an hour before and with whom he was hoping to ride away so they could consummate their marriage. He hoisted her in the air, holding his bride by the waist with strong hands, and set her down on the justice of the peace's desk, promising the laughing, singing guests that he would not let the bride get down until she kissed him. At that point, someone interrupts the merriment, bringing word of the noon train. And the ground caves in. Kelly abandons Cooper because he refuses to run from the killers. Then the song is heard again.

Sometimes, my father sang it to me, darkening his voice because he saw that I liked the sad song better that way, campfire-dark, as if a lonely cowboy were singing. He sang in German,

Warum bist du von mir gegangen . . .
Oh, why have you gone and left me?

I couldn't remember the rest of the words because at the time I always fixated on the word *gegangen*. It sounded so terrible, so final. The couple, whom I always secretly identified with my parents, had parted. One of them had deserted the other, irrevocably, once and for all. As my father sang, I saw the hero searching, saw him sitting by the fire under the empty night sky, staring into the flames and muttering the question. There was only this question, which went unanswered. He sang the question and left me dangling, with this final, hopelessly sorrowful *gegangen* in my ears.

I am sure I was afraid at the time that my parents might split up. The fear made my throat tighten and prevented me from remembering the rest of the song. Fear that my father was singing so beautifully, with such mournful loneliness, because he sensed that the song expressed his own destiny and, therefore, mine as well. Nonetheless, I loved hearing that song, I don't know why, and asked him again and again to sing it for me.

Warum bist du von mir gegangen?

It also seemed that the man by the campfire, my father and I, too, received some answer from the song after all. I saw Cooper, the solitary Cooper in *High Noon*, knocking on doors, asking for help but in vain. He has no choice but to walk down that street alone. Walk down the deserted street.

'They shot that film,' Rex was saying, 'a couple of miles east of here, on the Columbia Ranch in Burbank.'

'Really? *High Noon?*'

'In those days, they had all kinds of Western streets on the lot. "Hadleyville", a whole town.'

'Listen,' I said, 'I just remembered the song you heard at the beginning. I know it only in German but...'

Rex interrupted me, singing:

Do not forsake me, oh my darlin'...

'Of course Tex Ritter sings it better,' he added with a grin. Then he sang the line again:

Do not forsake me, oh my darlin'...

'It sounds much darker in German,' I said. 'He doesn't ask her not to leave him. She's already left him, and it tears him up; he can't understand why she would do that. How does the song go on in English, do you remember?'

Rex tried to reconstruct it. Tapping the table in four/four time, his hand soon captured the rhythm of a lone drum which, I recalled, clip-clopped for many measures like hoof beats, pursuing the voice from a distance.

> *Do not forsake me, oh my darlin'*
> *On this our weddin' day.*
> *Do not forsake me, oh my darlin'—*
> *Wait, wait along . . .*

'I don't remember the rest of it either,' Rex said. 'Tex Ritter was an old cowboy, you know, and he drawled the word *day*, as if the wedding day first had to pass through a deep valley with the cowboy before it finally climbed to a safe elevation, like his voice. He also stretched out *along*, as if the waiting they did together, I mean her waiting along with him, waiting for him and on his behalf—were their consummation.'

'Sorry, I have to get going now,' I said, pulling on my coat.

'Must you?' Rex asked, 'Already? It's raining so hard.'

'Well, my flight leaves at three and I should head for the airport at noon.'

'Your flight?'

'Yes, I have to go to Germany.'

'To Germany, man. And when will you be back?'

'In a couple of months, I think, at the end of July.'

At that—it came back to me later, as I thought about it—something in Rex changed. He insisted that I sit down again.

'Hey, just five more minutes, give me five more minutes,' he begged me. 'Just think, a couple of months before he died . . .'

'You mean your father?'

'Coop, man, Cooper. Gary Cooper,' Rex corrected me. 'It was February '61. Kennedy had been inaugurated a couple of weeks earlier. I was in a men's clothing store in Beverly Hills. On the corner of Wilshire and Beverly Drive. The shop belonged to Sol Hester. He carried the best men's jackets at the time. Sol looked like Peter Gunn, the coolest detective, and I . . .'

'Slow down, Rex, slow down. You're losing me.'

'Well, I'm there in the store, talking with Sol. I was teaching his wife, Helen, to drive at the time. I thought the world of her. She was from Mexico, Guadalajara, I think. Anyway, we were talking about her. Sol was asking questions that were making me more and more uncomfortable. I was trying to think how I could get out of there, when I heard the door chime. A customer, I thought: here's your chance to slip away. And then in comes . . . it's Gary Cooper who comes into the store. Suddenly, he's standing next to me. He nods. Shyly. I just stand there, completely frozen. Don't even respond. He was shy, seemed apologetic at interrupting. Then he speaks. Sol draws him to one side but there isn't much room in the shop. Cooper's only an arm's length away. The two of them are talking, Cooper in this low voice. He smiles at Sol and Sol listens. Something inconsequential, it seems to me. And I look at his hands, his large hands. They're spotted and, for that very reason, beautiful. He rests them on the glass counter of the display case. He's not there to buy anything, to pick anything up. Then he leaves. Sol—I'm still glued to the spot— Sol comes over to me, his face pale. And when he sees, over my shoulder, that Gary Cooper doesn't stop in front of the store—I turn to look: Cooper is crossing the street, towards Rodeo Drive—Sol leans towards me and whispers, "People know already." For a moment I was alarmed, thinking he was talking about Helen, that people had seen us together. That Gary Cooper was going to . . . But then Sol said, "We've known for several days." His voice was shaking. "Cooper is dying. Cancer." Yes, a few of Sol's friends who owned shops on Canon and Crescent Drive had given Sol the news several days earlier. Cooper had come by to see them, too. Hadn't bought anything or picked anything up. Just exchanged a few words with them. "He's saying goodbye, see," Sol said. "He doesn't mention being ill but what he means is goodbye. I'm sure we just saw Mr. Cooper for the last time." And Sol turned out to be right, you know. He never saw him again.'

Rex could tell that I was impressed, but really wanted to go now. Had to go. Suddenly he said, perhaps to stop me, 'So I followed him.'

'What do you mean?'

'I followed him,' Rex said again. 'I said goodbye to Sol, left the store, crossed the street in the direction Gary Cooper had gone.'

'And?'

'At the corner of Rodeo, by the Beverly Wilshire Hotel, I caught up with him. I stayed behind him, at a safe distance. I didn't want to bother him, just see where he was going. Keep him in sight. He went into another store, a stationery store, I think, on Rodeo Drive. I didn't follow him in, just looked through the window. I saw a salesgirl recognize him. She was tempted to run up to the great man, but she checked herself at the last moment, just rose on tiptoe, as if that was the only way she could balance her joy and her self-control, then spoke to him, asking how she could help. I saw her beckon and call out to someone. Saw her eyes cling in admiration to Cooper's face as he turned away and rather shyly took several steps towards the back of the store. An older lady came towards him, moving with some difficulty. You could tell she'd known Cooper for a long time. He didn't buy anything, didn't pick anything up. He also didn't accept anything. The lady had her heart set on giving him a gift. A fountain pen, I think it was. Whatever. He wouldn't take it. But his manner seemed to promise, "Next time." He winked as he walked past the salesgirl, who was now on the phone. I saw her ponytail swing to one side as she turned away, blushing, to share with a friend the news that the star of *Love in the Afternoon*, with Audrey Hepburn, was there in the store—"Oh my God, he just winked at me!"

'But Cooper had already left the shop, the expression on his face completely altered, I noticed.

'He visited two or three more shops where he'd been a regular customer. I knew Sol was right: "Cancer, dying, we've seen him for the last time." I knew because I could see that the man I was following knew. Knew with every step he took, with every inch of his body.

'Actually, it seemed to me, his visits down the streets of Beverly Hills were no different from those in *High Noon*. He was knocking, asking for help. As if the great star were waiting for someone to reach out to him, despite his heroic readiness to die, for someone to take his hand and say, "I'll go with you. You're not alone."

'Finally, he stopped next to a movie theater. Only then did I realize we'd gone in a circle. It was the movie theater with the Oriental dome near Sol's shop. Cooper seemed to hesitate, too, when he noticed that he was almost back at Sol's store. He looked at his watch and only then realized he was in front of a movie theater. *The Misfits* was playing. Marilyn Monroe, Montgomery Clift, Clark Gable. Gable had died only two or three months earlier. And Cooper and Gable knew each other well. Cooper looked at the poster, stepped shyly up to it, as if one of the names were hard to read. And didn't turn away until some people approached the theater. He moved across the sidewalk to the curb. Again he looked at his watch.

'Then someone on the street spoke to him. A woman, a moviegoer. She was about to buy a ticket, and had recognized him. She plainly wanted an autograph. She held something out to him, something to write on. A handkerchief. And then turned sideways, offering him her shoulder as a writing surface. He's completely flustered. I don't understand why. This must have happened to him thousands of times. He looks almost shamefaced as she stands there, offering him her back and shoulder and still holding out the handkerchief. He takes it, signs, then looks around. As he glances behind him, he sees me. He nods. Maybe he recognized me, I think. Surely he remembers seeing me earlier at Sol's, just a few steps down the street. Why not? I think. Why not me, too? Why don't I go to him and shake his hand? The hand my father once shook, you know? Before they switched, switched hands, and my father substituted his own hands for Cooper's. And why don't I say, "Mr. Cooper, what connects us through the years is . . ." And he'll remember, remember my father and the close-ups of the hands in *High Noon* . . .

'I go towards him. The moviegoer has just left. I say, quite loudly, so he'll hear me, "Mr. Cooper, my father . . ." At that moment a car pulls up to the curb next to him, a black limousine. He gets in but looks around at me. And lifts his hand, maybe to wave to me. Maybe also partly warding me off, to be honest: "No more autographs." It was hard to tell. I'd call it a wave. He had to get into the car after all. It was clear he'd been expecting it. Got in and rode off. It was . . . a wave, and if I'd come closer, we'd certainly have shaken hands. He'd already extended his towards me after all. Like a wave.'

'I understand,' I said. 'It would've been nice if you . . .' I didn't finish the sentence. Clearly, Rex had often thought back to this moment.

'Yes, it would've been nice,' he said, after a brief pause. His answer applied to us, too, because he saw I had to go. It was time.

I got up and deposited my tray on the counter, behind which Luz was stowing a tray of fresh bagels.

'See you,' I said to her. 'See you,' to Rex, and I raised my hand to wave.

For a moment, before I opened the door, I felt myself back in that dream about the arrival of the storm. As a dreamer, I had closed Noah's door in time, had managed to escape into the space that saved me.

Now I pushed the door open and stepped outside, hunching my shoulders. The wind had died down. I dashed home through the rain to the Starlite Terrace.

Two and a half months later, when I got back from Germany, I did not go by to see Rex right away. I had various things to take care of and it was only on the third or fourth day that I got to Noah's. It was early morning again, shortly after six. Pete was already seated by the window. He was sipping from his disposable cup when he saw me come in. I fetched bagels, jam and coffee, then went to our table and put my tray down.

'You've heard?' Pete said, not wanting to say the words.

Rex had died four weeks earlier in the hospital.

That day, the day when Pete and I had seen him for the last time, he'd gone for tests. It was cancer. They didn't want to let him leave. Had to operate right away. He went back to the Starlite, packed a few things, and called up Pete, who lived on the other side of the courtyard.

'Phoned me,' Pete said. 'That never happened before. Otherwise he always came by. I thought, by the way, there'd be all kinds of reproaches because I wouldn't go to the doctor's with him that morning, the way I usually did. But he didn't say a thing. He gave me the number of the hospital and said I should call in a couple of days. Not a single reproach. But he also didn't come by. I ran downstairs—his big blue beach towel was still lying by the pool in the rain—and knocked on his door. It opened; he always forgot to lock it . . .'

Pete looked at me, as if he wanted to be sure I believed him.

'I had a feeling,' he said. 'Not that he'd find out that day, but . . .'

'What about Rex?' I interrupted.

Pete shrugged. 'He'd left already. Shortly after the operation I went to the hospital,' he said. 'I wanted to check on him. He was still groggy from the anaesthesia. Or they'd given him painkillers. At any rate, he wasn't awake. Not really awake, not so you could talk to him. He didn't see me. Or at least didn't recognize me. When I went up to his ward, I heard someone screaming. Again and again. Screaming at the top of his lungs, like someone out in a storm. You could hear it one floor down. I asked, "What's going on here?" The nurses shrugged, as if there was nothing they could do. It was almost unbearable. How can Rex get better in all this racket, I thought?'

Pete brushed the crumbs off the table, his face troubled.

'I didn't realize it was Rex,' he said. 'Rex was screaming so hard that I didn't recognize his voice. Until I was standing outside his room. He was screaming, "THE KING IS DEAD . . . THE KING IS DEAD . . ." Over and over. Nothing else. "The king is dead." He stretched the words out as if he were dreaming. But he had his eyes wide open. Suddenly I knew it was true. His dream was a reality. As if we were all part of it. Of his dream. His downfall. Buried with him. As if we were all supposed to realize: "THE KING IS DEAD." Rex screamed as if he were being ripped apart. Believe me. Ripped apart before my eyes. The next day he was in a coma. Never came to.'

Half a year later, I found a small package in my mailbox, a gift from Artisan Home Entertainment for film critics. For the fiftieth anniversary of the 'four-category Oscar winner' Artisan had put together a collector's DVD version of *High Noon*.

My first impulse was to invite Pete over one evening, but then I watched the film alone, and afterwards, went out for a walk on Ventura Boulevard.

The hands of Rex's father—I had been waiting for them but the close-ups I thought I remembered were nowhere to be seen. There was only one close-up of Cooper's hands—when the marshal, before he makes his way down the street to meet his killers, writes his will.

'Last Will and Testament'. The words are formed with a scratchy pen on a white envelope by a large, handsome man's hand.

Cooper's hand, no doubt about it.

And what if it weren't, after all? I thought.

But watching for the missing close-ups spoiled my enjoyment of the film. I wished for my sake, and for Rex's, that something might be preserved here, something he had described, which belonged to him. His flesh and blood, so to speak, or at least a photographic image of it and the proof of . . . of what?

It occurred to me that Rex owed that story about his father's work as a hand double to a man who might have simply intended to comfort him. That extra who had come to the funeral when they buried Rex's father in Forest Lawn.

I remembered that cemetery on whose slopes D. W. Griffith had shot the Civil War scenes in his silent *Birth of a Nation*, and realized that, from there, you could see clear across to Burbank. And in the mid-fifties, down below along Pass Avenue, just a stone's throw from where today the Ventura Freeway cuts through, was the Columbia Ranch, with Hadleyville, the town in *High Noon* in which Rex's father was supposed to have served as Cooper's hand double.

Maybe that view suggested the idea on the spur of the moment to the man who wanted to comfort the boy at the graveside. The whole story. He could count on the fact that Rex hardly knew his father, had not seen him since he was seven. The man could have seized the occasion to immortalize the father, to bring him closer to Rex, so as to make the father's absence from his son's life more tolerable. Or . . .

Or it was all true.

As I passed Noah's, long since closed for the night, I realized that when I left the diner the year before we hadn't shaken hands, even though we'd just been speaking of such a missed opportunity.

I could not banish the thought that Rex might have told the story about himself and Cooper because he knew, already knew, that he had cancer and wanted to convey that to me somehow, at the latest when he learned I was about to get on a plane. And that I had failed to understand him, thinking I had merely heard a story. Rex knew he would not see me again. And forced himself to admit the truth, hard though it was, by telling me about Cooper's last rounds.

The wind sprang up, coming from the east, warm and dry, as if the advance guard of the red winds, the Santa Ana winds, were streaming into the valley from the canyons. I felt wretched. And guilty. Overcome by the loneliness, the hopelessness that had been the persistent theme of Rex's life.

It was my hopelessness as well, I knew. The conviction that the stories did not turn out well. That the efforts were always in vain. In Rex's life as in my own. In Cooper's life.

What were those films, after all? I mean, what good did they do that man as he stood by the curb, having said a few goodbyes, and waited for his car? Was it for films, for any one of those films, that he had worked all his life? Did any one of them now, in '61, when he knew he had only a few weeks to live, mean anything to him?

All that falls away, I thought, when you have such knowledge. I defy anyone to say that at such moments a film means anything.

Not a thing: it all falls through the sieve. The street is swept bare. A wind springs up and carries away everything with it. The end of days. The king dies, the abyss opens up.

Then, shortly after I had crossed the boulevard in the direction of Border's, my dream came back to me. In the very spot where I was walking now, I had seen the fallen clouds swirling, crowding each other, spinning faster and faster. Images came rushing towards me, images from that dream.

I saw myself lying on the ground again, my hands shielding my head, behind that wall at Noah's, the wall that in my dream had not existed. I saw Rex, far off, by the window. The storm was causing everything to quake. It tore at the window panes and the door, broke through their frames and seized the man at the window, until everything went dark, was ripped apart . . .

Only now did I see something, the image that had eluded me as I woke up. The image that flashed amid that berserk darkness; I saw it flash again, in its entirety, so that I had to seize hold of it. Stop it as it penetrated me. I saw myself on the floor in that darkened space and heard something coming up behind me. There was a smell, an animal smell. A bearskin shirt. Yet the sound was that of hooves. Coming nearer, ever nearer. And then someone stepped over me. And as my head was held in the vise of his legs, without looking up I raised my hand. And felt ratty fabric in my hand. Only then did I look. It was a prisoner stepping over me, in a dusty prison jumpsuit, covered with signs. Some of them fell off like dust, like dust falling out of capsules. And as it struck me, this dust full of signs, all my fear of perishing in the storm left me. I saw him, the one who had stepped over me, his elbow blurred in rapid motion, his hand above me tugging at the horse's bridle. The hooves clopped behind me, then in front of me, as it followed him. He left the space, and as he mounted the horse in Noah's, all became still. As still as if the storm itself had now been mounted. Then he rode off through the open window, heading east, out onto the street, where day was breaking.

What did all this mean? And why had these images, and the rider, come back to me only now?

I was still standing, as if in a dream, but strengthened by it. Who was the prisoner who had stepped over me, causing all my fear, all my desolation to leave me?

And who, by the way, was Rex? What was he to me that I had listened to him for so long, had wanted to find the scenes containing the hands? What did he mean to me that he had turned up in my dream? Only days before his death. And now again, half a year later. What did he mean to me, that he had appeared again, ripped apart by the storm?

Only Rex's death, it seemed to me, had brought the other one into view. Announced his coming. The rider in dusty prison garb, the captive stepping over me. The horse.

And what if I had listened to Rex that time at Noah's because I had a premonition that he was on the edge of the abyss? Not only that, but listened so closely, listened to Rex so breathlessly because I knew he was speaking of both himself and me. That it was my destiny being announced.

I understood that the story about Cooper that Rex had told me dissolved into nothingness. Like all stories. And that that would be my story. That nothing could be saved. By any story. The loneliness of the man who followed another lonely man, that was my loneliness. The tale of an impending death, that was mine. The terminal illness, our conversation, which circled, encircled us, coming towards me. And here, only moments before, had caught up with me.

It seemed I had recognized Rex, in his helplessness, his futile flight from death, his search for hands, as what was most my own. Which did not belong to me. Rather, I belonged to him, was at his mercy, without realizing it. For I lived him, daily, in his flight, his loneliness, his delusional and desperate search. No, on the contrary, he lived me. He was the darkness within. 'Rex Judaeorum'. Ridiculously deprived of others' understanding, wholly unaware. My dark god who had lived me darkly.

But was now ripped apart. Had perished. To make way for the new. That was what had been announced. And had been brought about by the one who stepped over me, the captive liberator.

As yet I hardly knew how to put any of this insight into words. Except that, with the strength of the dream still sustaining me, for the first time I was free of fear. And only a bit of fear returned as I began to sense that this, too, would not last. That this certainty, too, had to be left behind.

I headed west, in the flickering light of passing headlights. Into the wind, back to the Starlite Terrace.

Something else occurred to me. It was like one last word from the Rex I had known. In whom I now recognized myself. He had told me about it during that last morning at Noah's but as if in passing. We had not dwelled on it. I had even forgotten it. But the longer I weighed it, the more evidently it provided an answer to a life. Here was something that could not be ripped apart, it seemed. At the last moment, as one was falling—what if no one ever came to step over one (but he did come!)—one would have to think of it and there find fulfillment enough. Looking out at the rain, Rex had mentioned that one time when Cooper was a child in Montana, his mother had dragged him out of bed in the middle of the night. The river was overflowing, threatening to wash away their house. And the mother had grabbed the sleeping child, and on horseback he and his parents had escaped certain death. I thought it was their flight to which Rex wanted to call attention. Its resemblance to escapes in films, to last-minute rescues. I did not recognize Rex's real concern until talking about Cooper's childhood brought him back to his own, and he began talking about himself again.

'One time,' Rex recalled, 'I was lying in bed. I must have been only five or six, and I would always lie under the sheet, which I like to lift up and then let down . . . It came floating down over me like a parachute, a sky of threadbare blue fabric with a pattern of stars. And I did that again and again, never tired of it. And one time, I still remember it clearly, I was doing it again, and the sheet came down slowly over me. Suddenly, I felt fingernails dig into my belly and side and hold me in a tight grip. It scared me, and I pulled the sheet off my face to see who was there. It was my mother—and I laughed like crazy. We both laughed. A strange feeling. I still have it today. I don't see a face, but I still feel her fingernails pressing into my belly and making me laugh, once I realize that it's her.'

TWO

Solar Eclipse

Moss McCloud was expecting a visit from his daughter. That all the residents of Starlite Terrace knew.

'But she doesn't exist,' Pete told me when he ran into me on the steps of our apartment complex. It was the last weekend in December, and at this hour of the morning it was still dark. Pete was on his way to Noah's, and I had been looking up and down Dickens Street for any sign of a woman who had supposedly just left the building.

'From time to time, McCloud invents this daughter,' Pete muttered, as he stepped onto the dew-drenched grass and stomped towards the pink, weather-beaten Starlite Terrace sign.

It was only recently that I had met Moss, who occupied the small apartment next to the laundry room. A stage actor who had gone on to work for a Broadway casting agency, Moss had left New York years ago and moved to Los Angeles. We knew each other only by sight when one morning he approached me out of the blue at Noah's and told me he had run into Jack Palance the day before at Border's and Jack had remembered him. In the old days, when they were both performing in *Darkness at Noon*, the play based on Koestler's novel, Palance had tormented him, grilling him without mercy, but yesterday, at the bookstore, Palance had been remarkably friendly. 'A changed man,' Moss asserted, pulling an old black-and-white photo out of his wallet. It showed Jack Palance bending menacingly over a pale young man who had tripped on the stage and was gazing 'dramatically' into the camera. 'How long ago was that?' I must have asked Moss, because, as I recall, he paused only a moment to think, then replied, 'I can tell you exactly. That photo was taken on the evening of November 22, 1963. We'd debated whether we should go on at all. That was the day Kennedy was killed.'

On this particular morning, Moss had rung my bell early, perhaps because he saw a light in my apartment. He stared at me in helpless confusion, as if he had just awakened from a terrible dream. His daughter had knocked on his door, he said, and since the light switch by his bed did not work, he had fumbled around and failed to get to the door in time. 'No doubt she thought her daddy was still asleep and now she's already on the way back to her car,' Moss speculated. He asked whether I would mind taking a quick look outside, his legs were giving him trouble these days.

'He invents this daughter—to make himself feel better,' Pete commented as he shoved the small 'One-Bedroom Apt. for Rent' plaque that was sliding out of its holder back into the middle of the Starlite Terrace sign. Rex's old apartment was still vacant.

'Do you ever see Moss at Noah's?' I asked.

'He never gets there as early as I do. And if he does, he sits off in a corner, pretending to be engrossed in his manuscript. He goes to Noah's only because he's homesick for New York. He never talked to Rex and me. But you he seems to trust. By the way, I told him you were also a writer. I was hoping he'd tell you what he's working on. That I'd be interested to hear.'

Pete grinned and headed off to Noah's, his hands stuffed into his jacket pockets. His breath formed a white cloud in the darkness as he passed through the glow of a streetlight.

I went back into the complex and was just passing the pool in the inner courtyard when the automatic timer switched off the underwater illumination and the turquoise blue disappeared. On the far side of the pool, back where Moss' apartment was, I could see light. His door was still open. So he's waiting for me, I thought. He thinks I'm coming back with his daughter.

I headed for his door, calling out to him, but there was no answer.

As I stepped inside, I saw, on the sagging couch to the right of the door, a cardboard container of melted chocolate ice cream and a bag of Christmas cookies. The television was on, and the screen showed the profile of some retired CIA agent talking on Fox News about Islamic terrorism. I found myself remembering Pete's comment that Moss' principal form of nourishment was Dreyer's Chocolate Ice Cream.

Inside the apartment, a musty smell wafted towards me, and it was clear that no one had done any cleaning in years. The floor and every available surface were covered with yellowing manuscripts, legal documents, letters and magazines. The piles of paper, tipping or toppled over, left Moss little room to move around.

I called his name again. Meanwhile, a line in a handwritten letter poking out from a stack of magazines caught my eye. In blue ink the line read, 'For God's sake, don't give up on me, Moss.' An insect of some kind was crawling up the side of the paper.

'I'm over here,' I heard Moss say. He was kneeling at the entrance to the kitchenette, by the counter.

'Were you able to catch up with her?'

'No, there was no one outside the building when I got there. Only Pete on his way to Noah's.'

'You're sure? What am I going to do now?'

On the dark floor of the small kitchen, I could make out hundreds of pages of manuscript, scattered in all directions. Moss picked up one of them, then replaced it carefully.

'Good God, I must have bumped into the table when I was running to open the door for Amy. Knocked over the whole manuscript. My manuscript! How will I ever get these pages in order again?'

It was his life story, Moss explained. He had written it down for Amy, to let her know, as he was determined she should one day, that her father had sacrificed everything for her. Everything. That would put an end, once and for all, to the lies her mother had told about him, lies with which she had turned Amy against her father and poisoned their relationship.

Pete's got it wrong, I thought. This daughter does exist, though it was unlikely she had knocked on Moss' door just now.

'Do you have a picture of her?'

'Of Amy?'

He braced himself against the wall and struggled to his feet, holding on to the door jamb.

'I know,' Moss said, 'Pete claims I just imagine her. It may be true that I . . . that a few times I dreamed I heard the doorbell and Amy was standing outside. That's possible. But there are signs and portents for everything. Everything, buddy.'

Moss looked at me as though he were testing me, watching to see his words' effect.

'So . . .' he hesitated, 'can I trust you?'

'What do you mean?' I asked.

'You won't rat me out when they come?'

As he gazed at me, I saw he was trembling. Pete had mentioned that Moss was terrified of being taken to a nursing home. His stepsister, who lived in Gainesville, Florida and supported Moss financially, might insist on his being moved to a home—out of concern for his health.

'You mean the people who come to take you to a nursing home? Don't worry, Moss.'

Moss went to the door and closed it.

'Who knows how they'll identify themselves,' he said. 'Off to the home,' they may say. Those guys will even pack a suitcase for you. And then it's off to the showers. I tell you, those are coming back. These days, you don't even have to read between the lines.

Pete's clued in, too, by the way. I had no choice but to tell him. But if things reach that point, just follow them in. Don't be shy. They'll search the place but I'll happen not to be here. Tell them you expect me back in a couple of hours. Got it?'

I still had no idea what he was talking about. All I had done was ask whether he had a picture of his daughter.

Then Moss went to the closet in the wall opposite the kitchen counter. He beckoned to me.

Moss opened the closet, which was crammed with suits, ties and shirts, shoved them aside, and . . . stepped in. He kneeled, his back to me. For a moment it looked as though he were meditating or praying. Then he raised one arm and groped for something on the back wall. I saw the panel yield, swinging away. Moss beckoned to me again, stepped through the opening, and disappeared.

'Follow me!'

I stepped gingerly after him. On the other side of the wall it was dark.

'Wait,' I heard Moss saying, 'I'll turn on the light.'

Suddenly I saw—only three or four steps in front of me—the entrance to a dimly lit bedroom.

'This is where you sleep?'

'Sometimes,' Moss replied. 'Well, more and more often these days. It's safer here, in my "ark of bulrushes".'

On the floor of the small room lay a mattress with sheets, a couple of blankets and pillows. A lamp stood next to the mattress. In one corner, I saw a radio, a stuffed backpack, a three-gallon bottle of Arrowhead water, some cans of peaches and a partially eaten chocolate bar.

'Don't rat me out,' he repeated.

'Don't worry, Moss. But . . . is there any ventilation in here? In the summer, it must be like an oven.'

Moss patted the wall behind the backpack. 'There's a vent here. In a pinch, I can even crawl through. The freshest air comes in from the laundry room. I used to hear singing, too.

He made the night a little brighter
Wherever he would go,
The old lamplighter
Of long, long ago . . .

Rex used to sing that,' Moss said. 'He provided entertainment while he was folding his laundry.'

Moss hummed as he picked up the lamp. He held it to a framed picture hanging above the mattress at eye level.

'Is that . . .?'

'Amy,' Moss answered.

'How old is she there?'

'Three. That was on her third birthday,' he said, 'November 12. See how happy she is? We were still in New York then. In '66. She's offering me a picture she'd just drawn for me.'

Moss squatted down and pointed to a colored photocopy he had tacked to the wall at the head of the mattress.

'I keep the original in my backpack,' he said.

'A horse?'

'A horse *with blue wings*, if you please. She'd seen it on television, Pegasus. It was meant to protect me,' Moss explained proudly.

I turned and pointed to a photo of a child on the opposite wall, next to the passage to the closet. 'Is that her as well?'

Moss held the lamp close to the picture. 'No, no, that . . . that's a photo from a newspaper article. That's me, the kid with a bandaged head. But the puppy wasn't mine, I'm sorry to say. I don't know whose dachshund that was. Someone just placed it next to me when they were taking pictures for the paper. I'm three there. Like Amy. The two pictures are looking at each other, see?'

I tried to decipher the yellowed text next to the photo. It came from the *St Louis Post Dispatch*. The headline was still legible: 'Miracle Boy Survives Fall from Fourth Floor.'

'So what happened?'

'They say I fell out the window but that's ridiculous. I went back later to see for myself. There was no way I could have climbed onto the windowsill at three. No, I think my mother threw me out the window. In a rage. She'd been fighting with my stepfather. A reliable source told me. I don't know my real father. You'll laugh: he was a milkman . . . Yes. And Jewish, too. Marriage was out of the question. To avoid a scandal, they sent her to Vienna. So I was born there—though the official record says otherwise. All her life she suffered from depression, from migraines, from uncontrollable rages. I'm telling you, she threw me out that window. I landed on the sidewalk, head first. Dead. 'Dead,' is what the ambulance driver said when he got there. He didn't even want to put me on the stretcher, the good man. But the other paramedic insisted on loading me in the ambulance and taking me to the hospital—God only knows why; I must have looked awful. I never found out his name, the man I owe my life to. At any rate, as you see there, I was back on my feet in three weeks, and they sent me home. With that bandage. Look!'

Moss pointed to his forehead, above his shaggy right eyebrow. A thin line, a bit paler than the rest of his skin, ran on an angle to the base of his nose and angled up sharply.

'Go ahead, feel it,' Moss urged me.

When I put my finger on the scar, the skin gave way alarmingly.

'There's no bone under there,' Moss explained, laughing. 'That was my brain you just tickled. The fact the doctors left it unprotected like that saved my life a number of times, or so I would say today. There were periods when I was in such despair over my situation that I wanted to volunteer for whatever war we happened to be fighting—Korea, even Cuba, Vietnam. But each time they turned me down. "4F".' Moss pressed a finger into his forehead. 'Nothing doing.'

A little later, I made my way back to my apartment, saddened and shaken by what I had just seen and heard. 'Here, feel how heavy this is,' he had said when we returned to his living room and he'd picked up a random pile of manuscript and pressed it into my hands. 'It certainly is,' I'd replied. 'Take it with you,' he'd urged me, 'I can't read it anymore. My eyes are giving out.' 'Not right now,' I'd said and was relieved when he took the manuscript back.

Hoping to distract myself from the image of the lonely old man living amid that chaos of papers, tormented by anxiety and filled with unjustified anticipation, I climbed back into bed and switched on the television. Outside the sky was turning gray.

Key Largo had already started. A hurricane was approaching the southern coast of Florida. Karl Freund's cinematography captured the chalky gray light presaging a storm while Bogart helped Lauren Bacall tie up the boat at the pier. At the hotel, Edward G. Robinson was holed up with his gangsters. Robinson was Johnny Rocco, who had left his Cuban exile and had chugged to the Keys in his boat to close a deal. The gangster was homesick for America. But, at this point, Bogart has no idea what kind of person he's dealing with. He has just met Bacall and from the bow he tosses the rope across the water to her. Bacall, on the pier, catches the rope and places the loop over one of the bollards. And then . . . then Bogart uses the same rope to pull himself over the gap, along with the boat and me, back to Bacall. What a feat, to glide along, pulling and being pulled at the same time. The three or four yards over the water . . . back to the landing. Where Bacall is waiting. Bogart climbs into her frame, up to the dock, and then the two of them stand there together in a two-shot. Now the storm can come.

During the commercial I dozed off. Moments before I had been thinking about my parents and the way they met on Heidelberg's main street, near the corner by the Grain Market, around the same time as Bacall and Bogart were filming the scene on the dock in the Warner Brothers' studio. Had my father and his friend left the Red Ox only a few seconds later, had they paid their check only two or three seconds later, or, alternatively, buttoned their coats faster —a storm was gathering outside—and reached the Grain Market corner two or three seconds earlier . . . I would not have been there to join Bacall on the pier.

I dozed off. It seems to me in my dream that I have just woken up. I try to switch on my bedside lamp but it won't go on. The room stays dark. Everything is silent, and suddenly it becomes clear to me that something is wrong with the fuse. No power in the whole apartment. In my dream it comes to me that Moss mentioned his light switch was broken, too. I make my way towards the closed curtains, sensing that the reason everything is so quiet outside is that it may have snowed. As I stand by the curtain and am about to lift one corner and peep outside, the woman standing behind me on the right seems very familiar. She woke up with me, I realize. A pleasant feeling to have her so close. I move a bit to one side to let her see out. A very faint, high tone can be heard, hovering in the air, like the 'Aaaaah' sound remembered from childhood visits to the theater when the curtain rises. And in fact it looks to us at first as if the street outside is buried in snow. All this must have happened while we were sleeping, we think. Then in my dream I realize that what I am seeing is a raging torrent, not snow but chalky white rain water rushing by—yet it isn't raining, no, it rained earlier, the rain cascaded down from the hills, is flooding at a terrific speed along the street and past our building. And then, down below, by our building, on our side of the water, someone is trying to cross the street. Not possible! I think. How can he prevail against the crushing power of the water? He looks like Bogart, but then I recognize Moss; his disheveled hair and the scar on his forehead give him away. As I watch, Moss tosses a rope into the rushing stream. It wraps itself around a blue fender floating by in the water. Moss tries to haul it to land, but the current pulls him into the water. Now he is balancing on the piece of sheet metal, being swept along! It all happens so quickly that it is almost comical. For a little while, we can still see him but by the time he gets to the corner of Cedros, our eyes can no longer make him out.

A few days later, when the evening rush hour was already in full swing, I ran into Moss at the intersection of Kester and Ventura Boulevard. He was distraught, muttering to himself.

I learned that a few hours earlier he had biked to Border's and had left his bike behind the hedge in front of the store. He had gone inside, had listened to music upstairs at one of the listening stations, had had a cup of coffee and looked at a few books. That was all. Not until he was making his way back through the store did it occur to him that he had left his manuscript—painstakingly picked up from the floor, put in order and stowed in two file cases—in the basket on the front of his bike. When he got outside, it was gone. Not a trace of the bicycle or the manuscript.

'Because you didn't actually park your bike there,' I said. 'Am I right?'

I could tell he wished I were.

'But . . . that's the only place I went, I swear,' Moss replied. 'I went straight from home to the bookstore.'

'So you're sure of that?'

'Yes, I'm sure . . . If I lose the manuscript now, it's all over. If I've lost it, I'm putting an end to this charade.'

'Who'd steal a bike like yours?' I asked him. 'Only a kid. And he'll abandon it sooner rather than later.'

'You think so?'

'It's quite likely.'

For a good hour we searched all the streets around Border's, from Willis Avenue to Camarillo, and back to Hortense Street by way of Natick. Then Cedros, Vesper and Vista del Monte. Moss pointed out the house where Marilyn Monroe spent her first wedding night. Sixteen she was at the time. She called her husband Daddy, Moss told me. 'The first photographer she worked with stole her from him.'

Along the sidewalk people had put out Christmas trees for the trash pick-up. In my mind's eye, I kept seeing the foolish image of a child's bike lying on the ground. In movies made in the fifties, the father sees a bike as he turns into the driveway of his single-family home. Smiling, he picks it up and parks it neatly by the front door. Did such things ever happen in real life? Certainly they no longer did.

Shortly before sunset, Moss and I were walking down the long alley behind the Ventura Boulevard shops. We should have looked here first, we agreed. Whoever had stolen the bike would have turned first onto this nameless side street—to be out of sight. Then would have ditched the manuscript. And tossed the file cases somewhere. Into one of the garbage cans or bins behind the shops.

Moss was still in utter despair. The accumulated memories of the past twenty years, the whole story he wanted to place in Amy's hands some day, to justify himself once and for all to his child . . . And now he had been robbed again.

'She's the one who stole it, you know?' Moss remarked as he held the rickety crate I had climbed onto in order to shine the flashlight we had borrowed from Luz at Noah's into a large trash bin. Nothing but garbage and discarded Christmas decorations.

'Who do you mean?' I asked.

'My wife. She stole Amy from me. Back in '66. Kidnapped her. Took off. Was gone from one day to the next. I was a casting agent at the time. On Broadway. Had been working there for a couple of years already. Not a struggling actor any more. I was making a good living. We had a five-room apartment across from Central Park. And she had a fantastic job. Stella was an actress and she was appearing in an Edward Albee play. That's where she must have met him. He was a TV writer, came from L.A., was just visiting New York. But all that I found out only later. One evening, I come home, suspecting nothing. No letter, no note. My neighbor says he saw her getting into a cab with a ton of suitcases. Her and the child. They were heading for Grand Central, that much he was able to pick up. My lawyer tried to calm me down; he wanted to do some investigating. Days passed. My nerves were shot. Stella had never been any good with the child, you know. Too strict for my taste. In some respects, she reminded me of my mother. I thought Amy might really be in danger. I mean, who's crazy enough to run away like that? After three years of marriage! Without a word, without warning—and leaving not a single trace. Robbing me of the thing that means the most to me in the whole world, this child. She knew that was the way to get to me, to deliver a deadly blow.

'One evening—two weeks had passed, I think, without any word from her, and still not a trace of them—when I was meeting some people in connection with my work, they invited me to come along to a dinner party. I said no, I'm not up to it. But they insisted.

'An hour later I was feeling better. The other guests had all listened to me. Amazing: every one of them. The host and his wife were writers from L.A.. They'd rented an apartment in New York while they were doing research, I heard, for a movie. A story about the New York Mafia. Burt Lancaster's name was mentioned, as was Anthony Quinn's. But mostly everyone listened to me. With great interest and lots of sympathy. I bewailed my plight. "Can any of you understand?" Yes, they could. They showed genuine compassion.

'When dinner was over, everyone got up. Only one person remained seated. Too drunk to move, I thought. I was also . . . I'd had a few. The guy sitting at the corner of the table across from me was around forty-five. Not much bigger than me but with a powerful build. Up to now, I realized, he'd hardly said a word. Only listened. To me and the others. Now he looked straight at me—some of the guests were leaving, others standing by the bar with the host—now he looked straight at me and said, "Why don't you take out a contract on her?" "A contract?" I asked incredulously. "Sure. Happens all the time," he replied. "One day she doesn't come home from work. After that it won't be long before you have your little darling back." I asked whether he was serious . . . "I thought *you* were serious," he answered. "Yes, but . . . ," I say, "but that's crazy. They'd figure out right away who . . ." "That's what they wouldn't figure out. You haven't figured it out yourself. You don't know anything. Right now, you don't even know where she's gone with your kid." That was true: I had no idea. "It'll cost you five hundred bucks," he continued. "We need a picture, the name and number on her driver's license. You pay, and that's it as far as you're concerned. The money passes through fifty hands in, let's say, thirty states. No one knows who ordered the hit. One day you get word that you're to come pick up your daughter. That should put a stop to your whining."'

'Can you imagine?' Moss continued, 'I actually considered it. I mean, you can't imagine how humiliated I was. And at the same time terribly worried about Amy. "Think it over," the man said. He gave me the name of an Italian restaurant in the Bronx, Da Bruno, on Tremont Avenue. He'd be having lunch there on Friday. "You go in, sit down, order some food. Then you go to the restroom. When I come in, you give me the five hundred, and return to your table. That's it." The man got up and went to say goodbye to the hosts. I didn't even know his name. But I was sure, absolutely sure, you know, that he would get the job done. I could give him the money and the problem would be solved.

'The next morning—I'd slept horribly—the whole thing seemed utterly crazy. But towards noon, after I'd checked with my lawyer, who had no new information, nothing on Stella's and Amy's whereabouts, I began toying with the idea again. I wasn't sure how long I could keep going. My nerves were shot. Work was almost out of the question. Imaginary scenarios preoccupied me. "It'll pass through thirty states, fifty hands," the man had said. I could see him before me, his strong hands, which would write my wife's name and driver's license number on the back of her photo. Would stick it in an envelope. Toss into the mail, I thought. No phone call. Someone would open the envelope. Where? Somewhere. Outside the sun is shining, and this next man, who doesn't know he's number two—or how does this work? Does he know? At any rate, he sets down his coffee cup next to the photo and balances his lighted cigarette on the saucer. Does he look at the photo? Yes, but just for a second. The next man will take a longer look, I thought. Maybe in Duluth, Minnesota. He has nothing better to do. It's raining there. He knows the mail came from . . . it's postmarked Ithaca, New York. "Ithaca," he thinks. "That's where I had a thing with that woman called Betty." And he looks at the photo and thinks, "She looks a little like her." And then the next guy, the . . . fourth, where does he live? With his mother. She brings him the mail. The paper, the *St. Louis Post Dispatch*, and a letter from . . . The rain has blurred everything. The rain in Duluth, Minnesota. No one can make out the postmark. No matter. The guy in St. Louis isn't the one, either. Just sends it on to . . . Flagstaff, Arizona, or to Montgomery, Alabama, Monroe, Arkansas, to Pueblo, Colorado, to, hey, why not, Gainesville, Florida, where a driver in a midnight-blue Buick waves at my stepsister over the crosswalk. On the passenger's side, the photo is lying under a pack of cigarettes and a heavy bunch of keys. And three days later, in Wallace, Idaho, a man is splashing cold water on his face after a night of boozing in Spokane. He gives the photo to a young fellow whose girlfriend he plans to make a move on in the next few days. I see the young fellow in a diner somewhere along the highway. It's nighttime, he's exhausted, has just ordered, and is thinking about his girl. He hasn't a clue. He has some time while he waits for his steak with eggs over easy. Coffee. The waitress refills his cup. He wipes his mouth with the paper napkin. He pays on the way out. A brown envelope falls out of his pocket as he takes out his wallet. He picks it up, stuffs it in his side pocket. Pulls a twenty out of the wallet. As he does so, I can see five crisp hundred-dollar bills tucked in next to it.

'Whole chains of images like these kept passing before my eyes. As if to reassure me: "No one's going to make the connection with you. Completely impossible. No evidence will point to you." The trail—that was the tantalizingly reassuring part of these imaginings—the trail got lost in a thicket of details, in these clichés of gangsters. Details with which I would have had no contact, ever. I couldn't conceive what that really meant: "pass through fifty hands, in thirty states". How did that work? I had no idea. But you conjure up an endless network, one that extends so far that you lose track. Lose track of the fact that it started with you.

'I wouldn't know anything, I told myself. The whole process would take on a life of its own.

'The next day—it was the day before the appointed one—I scraped together the money. Normally, I would have had that much on hand, or at least two or three hundred. But she'd taken the money, too. A couple of actors owed me fifty or sixty dollars, I withdrew another hundred from the bank, borrowed fifty more from various people, and so on. At least I was careful not to give myself away. Even when I was toying with the idea of going through with it. Careful.

'I thought: What's to prevent me from checking out the restaurant a day early, having a meal where I was to meet him tomorrow? Can I do that? Could I do that? How would it feel? How does it feel when you go there, do the deed and leave? And once more—I was already on my way—the whole business seemed completely insane. It wasn't just the plan that was insane, it was the very thought. You're not going through with this, Moss McCloud. You won't do it because . . . and here my fear crystallized: because they'll catch you. Very simple. Still: if someone . . . if someone would guarantee that . . . but no one can do that. No one can do that because no one can guarantee anything. And because no one knows about it. No one knows when, where . . . Who would want to give me a guarantee? Well, for that very reason, I told myself, it could actually work.

'Suddenly, I was standing in front of the restaurant. The smells wafting onto the street were very good and I was famished. I went inside, sat down at a free table. And ordered. Looked at the other diners, classic types. If one of them had objected to my staring, I could have placated him. In those days I always had complimentary tickets on me. And who would be offended if you told him you were thinking of casting him in a Broadway play? I was enjoying my food and was almost finished when it occurred to me that this was a last meal of sorts. Or at least could be. If I took the plunge the next day and came back with the money . . . a last meal. A last something. Something final. I got up and went to the men's room. I had almost forgotten that part. I was alone in the men's room. Stood there. Washed my hands. Pictured myself—I reached into my pocket— handing him the money. Quickly, painlessly. No envelope. Nothing to get in the way of his counting it then and there. If he wanted to. No one would see. He'd go into the stall. And in the meantime I'd wash my hands. Dry them thoroughly. Back to the dining room.

'I paid the check and made my way home by a roundabout route. Thinking: All right, how did that feel? Answer: Not that bad. Really. Besides, I had all kinds of things to attend to. Appointments. I had no time for complicated thoughts. And wouldn't have the next day, either. It was . . . a normal day. And tomorrow would be a normal day, too. On the weekend, now, that might be different. That was when it would hit home. OK, but you could arrange to be with people. There was no shortage of actors and actresses dying to meet me. Invitations arrived daily. Most of them I turned down. But . . . what if there were problems? If my nerves got the best of me . . . tomorrow, after lunch? Well, I could let down my guard, accept a couple of invitations, I thought. Just to help me over the hump. And also to let myself be seen. I could take Harold along to a few events. My lawyer. Why not? A boring guy and later— but that's something I didn't find out right away— he really made colossal mistakes. Harold always wanted to meet people, especially women. A boring guy but, in that respect, insatiable. I'd get through the next few weeks somehow. Then, I was certain, after some time had passed, it would be as though nothing had happened. And not until the call came . . . the call. That I couldn't avoid. I had to be ready.

'The night before the rendezvous I didn't sleep a wink. Or at least that was how it felt. The next morning I was a wreck. Had a dim memory of an awful dream. Something sinister. I'd gone down to a cellar with a Mafioso. I knew it was a cellar in his house. And he pulls on a string, turning on a naked bulb. And then he bends backward—in this harsh light— hollowing out his back, supporting himself on some crates, which slip back a little, making a terrible grating sound. Yes, he bends backward, positioning his throat under the light, offering it to me. And in my dream, I know that I have to cut my finger. Cutting your finger is part of the ritual here. I have to hold my bleeding finger over him, over this guy, who will open his mouth. And my blood has to drip into it. And as he receives my blood and swallows it, I know I have been made. Am one of them. An awful dream.

'I went to work, determined to forget the whole business. No sooner had I arrived at the office than my secretary told me that the producer I was scheduled to see at two o'clock had canceled, and we should try to move something else into that time slot. But then I hear myself saying, "No, don't bother. I'm going out for lunch. I'll be back around three." The rendezvous was to take place at one o'clock. And just before twelve-thirty, I set out. I had to hurry.

Took a cab. We made good time at first. But then, of course, we hit traffic. I paid and got out. Started to run. I knew it wasn't far. Just around the next corner. I pass a bank and see my reflection in the plate-glass window: rushing towards my destination, my hand in my pants pockets, Sinatra-style. And—I realized—completely insane. The large pane provided just enough of a reflection, the light was right for me to catch a glimpse of myself. And I stopped. Stopped dead. Looked at myself in that sea of glass. Saw my eyes . . . the eyes of a stranger staring back at me. I was so unrecognizable that it horrified me. I turned away, just a half turn. To the door. Took one step . . . then another . . . went into the bank, made my way to the teller, and deposited the money. The whole five hundred. Into my account. Took the stamped deposit slip and stuck it in my wallet. Just to remind myself of how close I'd come. To remind God and myself. To remind Him of how close He had let me come. But also myself that at this moment I was sacrificing any certainty of seeing my daughter again—the stamped slip represented proof, if you like, of my pact with Him. I was making this sacrifice because well, . . . in the last analysis, of my own free will. I had seen something. Crazy, that reflection. Put there to let Him see the truth. *He* was the crazy one. I think He saw Himself in me. At this moment. Saw Himself in my plans—and was prepared to empty out His vessel of anger. *That's* what I had recognized.

'I hurried out of the bank and knew in my heart: now you're free of that. That and the rest, too. And I can tell you, the pain I felt at the thought that I might never see Amy again is something I wouldn't wish on anyone.

'I kept walking, passing the spot that had decided everything. The sun was at a different angle now, or maybe a cloud was blocking it. At any rate, nothing caught my attention—this time. I'd glanced at the bank window, because I . . . because I wanted to see again what I'd recognized. But, as I said, the window was no longer reflecting. The light had changed. It can't have been that I no longer had the money. So I passed the spot, then forced myself around the next corner. Instead of turning back and catching the first cab, you understand. Walked to the corner and made the turn.

'The restaurant where we were supposed to meet was only a block away. I headed in that direction. Should I really do this? I wondered. What if he recognizes me as I walk past? Runs after me? Ridiculous, complete nonsense! Nonetheless, I stopped. And then I saw—no more than twenty or thirty yards away—a small crowd gathering. And on the other side of the street, a photographer. He'd taken pictures for me once but I hadn't heard from him in a long time. He runs across the street and I go up to him: "What's happening down there?" He said he'd received a phone call. "Come with me, let's go and see!" And we're allowed through. The police haven't arrived yet but we can hear sirens approaching. Now I'm standing at the entrance to the restaurant, at the very spot where I stood the previous day, before I went in and looked for a table ... The diners motionless, still in shock. I see blood on the floor, a pool that's growing, see two men lying there. One of them I recognize immediately. Yes, the one I was supposed to meet. He must have been some kind of bodyguard. And the other one ... I don't recall his name. A man had come in, fired three or four shots, then left the restaurant. And by the table over there—they'd been sitting at the same table as the victims—stood ... my hosts from two days ago, the woman hysterical, her dress spattered with blood ... not *her* blood, no, not hers. The people whose dinner party I'd attended. They'd been having lunch with one of these men, a Mafioso they'd met in the course of doing research for their screenplay.

'The whole thing had gone down not five minutes earlier. My knees still tremble when I remind myself of that. This mob hit, as it was later described in the papers, had taken place no more than five minutes ago. If the light striking the bank's window, if that cloud in the sky had passed over the sun . . . just imagine . . . what a crazy thought! . . . if the wind driving the cloud had been a bit stronger and the sun had been hidden a moment sooner . . . I wouldn't have stopped, wouldn't have seen anything in the window, or at least not enough to stop me in my tracks. I'd have gone around the corner and—entered the restaurant just as it was happening.'

'And that's what you described in your manuscript for Amy?' I asked Moss.

'Yes. The plain truth,' Moss replied. 'I didn't want Amy to think I was trying to make myself look good. I had these thoughts, I had this opportunity, I struggled with the decision, and I made it. She has to know that. She has to know how far a person . . . no, how far I, her father, almost went. Can you understand that? Later I asked myself: What would have happened if I'd given the man . . . if I'd borrowed the money right away from the people who dragged me to that party? Then everything would have been taken care of that very evening. Such things happen, another man might not have hesitated. And he would have had a chance, a good chance, not to lose what I lost. You can't imagine. This whole business had enormous consequences.

'Two or three days after the rendezvous, or after that bloodbath, I heard from Harold, my lawyer. He'd found them. Amy and my wife—and the man with whom she'd run away to L.A..

'So I learned who it was. He had a house in Brentwood, topnotch lawyers, a good name in the industry, which at the time didn't make me jealous—I had a good name myself. But in the end what did a man's name mean if he took away another man's wife, and his child, too, why not, to keep her happy. He had plenty of money, and two children from a previous marriage. A hard worker, but not a workaholic, people said, known for being punctual and reliable when it came to getting a job done. Always knew what was hip, what was in—I think he was involved in the *Monkees* series, which was playing on TV at the time. Well liked, and in the right circles. An Emmy, a couple of Golden Globes on his mantelpiece, a beach house in Malibu. Occasional drug use—not the hard stuff—"and nothing that can be proved, so not usable in a custody challenge," Harold told me.

'For the time being, I focused on other matters. I'd done the right thing, I thought. I'd prevented a murder, or that was how it could be seen. I had the locks to our apartment on Central Park changed, moved out, taking a room in a small hotel, and sent Stella the new keys. "Here, these are for you, the whole apartment belongs to you and the child," I wrote. "But please come back. Do it for Amy. Come back to New York." Nothing. No reply, no reaction at all. She didn't take me up on it. And, as I said, she had better lawyers, as became clear to me. I should have changed mine but Harold stalled me. Finally, he convinced me that it would look better—in court—if I had an apartment in Los Angeles. For the child's sake. You can't ask a child to get on a plane every weekend. Her lawyers, it's true, told me from the beginning: "You're never going to see Amy again. Let it go, spare yourself the aggravation." The aggravation? Yes, everything was going downhill, I don't even remember why, or what the specifics were. My agency wasn't getting the right contracts any more. It was my fault, no doubt about it, nothing interested me, God knows, I was preoccupied with other things. Suddenly, the money was gone and I had to sell the apartment on Central Park. I'd bought it for five thousand dollars. Now I got a hundred twenty-five thousand for it. Who knows what it would be worth today. Two or three million at least.

'And I lost everything. Risked everything and lost it all. Over the years, I must have spent more than a hundred thousand on lawyers.

'I moved to L.A., first to Beverly Hills, then to Studio City, and for the last fifteen years I've been here in Sherman Oaks. At first it looked as though things would turn out all right for me. The court recognized the trouble I'd gone to. Saw that I'd sold everything and followed the wife who'd abandoned me and taken the child. All so I could see my daughter now and then. Three days a week. That was the deal. The judge's ruling. By now Amy was seven. Seven . . . And it went fine for a year.

'Then my wife, my ex-wife, came out with this terrible . . . this terrible accusation. Someone must have suggested it to her. "Just do that, and he'll be forced to clear himself. In the end they'll rule in your favor. Some suspicion always sticks." She accused me of molesting Amy. Took me to court with that lie! That's when I lost her—never saw her again. It's true that one time I did ask Amy to rub my back. So what? It was hurting and it made me feel better when she massaged it a bit. So what? I ask you, so what? One time I kissed her goodnight . . . Good God, I always kissed her goodnight. I loved her, always loved her, that child was everything to me. She was in bed and the blanket had slid off her leg, and I kissed her on the thigh, then pulled the blanket over her. That's all. One time. Completely innocuous. But her mother must have made a point of grilling her every time she came back from a visit: "Amy, does Daddy kiss you? OK, where does he kiss you?"

'So she took Amy from me. The court ruled in her favor and I'd lost once and for all.

'And it hurts so much when I consider that Amy might . . . I mean, it's imperative that she know there was no abuse, that I always loved her, that her mother tried to turn her against me with all kinds of lies, that I risked everything. And would do so again. You know what? I'd do it again. At least I think so. I'd spend all the money and try to get her back. What else could I do? What choice would I have? On the other hand, my wife can praise her lucky stars that that after-dinner conversation in New York . . . that it didn't take place after she accused me of abuse. She really lucked out. We all lucked out, I think.'

'And you never ran into her? Your wife? I mean, just by chance?'

'No, I never ran into her again. She had a success-ful career—it's the ultimate irony and tells you more about Hollywood than about her—as a TV writer. And the woman couldn't write! She couldn't even write a check! And won an Emmy. I assume *he* wrote the script and put her name on the title page, maybe for tax reasons, what do I know? And bam! That's how it goes. Another Emmy on the mantelpiece. She can't put two sentences together, that woman. No, thank God I never ran into her again. By the way, after the first time, the first time we saw each other, the same thing happened. I thought it just wasn't meant to be, wasn't meant to lead to anything. The whole story was completely crazy. As I said, there are always signs and portents. But that I already knew at the time. At the time! That was . . . wait, it was in '62. It must have been August. Shortly after Marilyn died. In '62 I was still an actor. That's what I was until just before Amy was born. Then I gave it up. Things went quite well for me. A casting agent offered me a job in his agency, taught me the ropes.

'All right, so at the time I was still an actor. I went for an audition. I still remember the play . . . It was that Wilder play, *Our Town*. George and . . . what was the name of the female lead? George and Emily, that was it. We were both auditioning, Stella and I. We didn't know each other yet, but . . . the two of us were assigned a scene. "Sit down in the corner there, and we'll call you in." We had ten minutes to rehearse together, to go over our lines. *Our Town*—I haven't the faintest idea why they would still be putting on that play in the sixties. Oh well, it was the *early* six-ties . . . At any rate, we sat down and read through the scene. The one in the drugstore. We come in, sit down, I order something for us . . . and she waits for me to declare my love. That's how I think it went— I'm not so sure anymore. At any rate . . . there we were, huddled in our corner. She was very friendly. I'd left my glasses at home, and was having a hard time making out the text. She read it to me, without getting impatient. And kept saying, "Look at *me*. Forget the text. The others will forget it, too, if we really wow them. If they can feel what's between us." And the minute we got through the scene, we started again. And there was something happening between us, no doubt about it. She looked into my eyes and there was something there. I've no idea what she saw. My God, Stella, what did you see back then? What madness life is. Stella looked at me, I spoke to her, said . . . what George says, that I won't leave our town, won't look for a job anywhere else, because . . . why should I? I've found everything I was looking for. Here, you . . . And more I don't want. All I want is you. And at that—I'm telling you—she gives me a kiss. It was . . . I never . . . man, this is crazy! That I'm remembering it now, under these circumstances . . . But I don't think I ever experienced anything like that again. It wasn't in the script, that kiss Emily gave George. And she . . . it wasn't a fleeting kiss, not at all. She moved her face a little, tilted it towards me, and suddenly she was very close. Intentionally, provocatively close. And then she gave me that kiss. And the kiss was, how should I put it, filled with infinite gratitude for what I'd just said. The lines

George . . . has to speak. Now that I've found you, I never want to leave. Her answer came in the form of that kiss. Her gratitude was . . . was erotic, you know? Gratitude for having been really understood. As if up to then finding understanding had been only a hope. Gratitude that she'd arrived, finally. That her life had become real.

'I . . . both of us, we were swept off our feet. Our ears were burning when they called us in for our audition.

'I have no idea what they thought of us. We were probably speaking much too softly. From the beginning. Paying no attention to technique. Still completely under the spell of what we'd . . . accomplished outside. And what had we accomplished? What did it mean? Damn, what wouldn't I give to know. What in the world was it? The directors interrupted us several times—"Louder, please!"—then sent us on our way. It was clear—we didn't have a shot. But . . . I couldn't get that woman out of my mind. I was besotted with her, as you can imagine, so bowled over by what had happened in that moment that when I walked her to the bus I didn't even ask for her phone number. I didn't know her name. Or did I? Did I know it already? Doesn't matter. At any rate I didn't have a phone number or an address. The number of the bus, yes. But it was long gone.

'And that was it. That would have been it. No, that's how it should have been. And I'd still remember that moment, that instant. Even if I'd never seen Stella again.

'And then . . . wait, one or two months passed. It was October. I'd just turned . . . thirty-three. We all thought our final hour had struck. Literally. It was during the Cuban missile crisis. During that one week in October '62, the crisis was building from day to day. Kennedy had found out that the Russians had installed launch pads for mid-range missiles in Cuba. "They can reach every city, every larger city in North and South America from there," we heard. "Nuclear war." And about twenty Russian ships and submarines were on their way to deliver more rockets. That was the situation. And Kennedy says, "Stop." And takes the whole thing to the American people. A major address on television, speeches on the radio. We see what's going on, or—as always—think we see what's going on. He orders a blockade of Cuba. Nothing can get through, not a ship, not a plane, we're told. And in the meantime, the Russian ships are streaming towards us. I mean, towards the blockade. A confrontation is inevitable. Tomorrow, we say, or some time tonight. Then all hell will break loose. Because no one can back down. *High Noon* off the shores of Cuba. And we've known this for days. We've lived it. And we sense that

91

it can't turn out well. Khrushchev, those Reds, they'll stop at nothing. Reds, that says it all. They're going to go ahead and press the button. Everyone is sure of that. All over. Just when things were looking up! Better days, freedom just around the corner. All over, the end of the world. Bombs will be dropped, the first on New York. Everyone's glued to the television, to the radio, hoping and praying that maybe, just maybe. . . But most people can feel it in their bones: this time we've had it, we won't get out of this alive. And some of us go to the Plaza that evening. The fanciest hotel in New York. I'm there with a woman I know and a few close friends. We decide to get totally smashed. In the Oak Room, dark and elegant and far too expensive for us. But what does that matter? No one will live past this night. We're convinced of that. Completely convinced.

'So we're sitting in the Plaza, our whole group at one table, and the other tables are all full, too. People have accepted the situation. They're with their best friends, ordering glass after glass. And listening to the radio. Everywhere in the Oak Room radios have been set up. No television. Radios. So we listen, talk about the impending nuclear war; any minute may be our last. And on the radio they keep reporting how far the Russian boats are from the blockade line. So you can calculate when the first boats will get there. "Another 425 miles . . . 354 miles . . . 290 . . . only

175 . . ." Unbelievably nerve-wracking. And we're downing one martini after another. I don't recall how long this went on, because . . . at some point I stood up. I wasn't properly drunk yet. I'd had a bite to eat beforehand . . . Maybe it was the excitement, the adrenalin. Anyway, I got up and headed for the men's room. And passed a table, one of the tables on the other side of the room. And there she sat. Stella. With a couple of men, a couple of girlfriends. And she saw me, too, saw me immediately. She was all dressed up. Something black and white, don't ask me . . . It rustled softly when she turned her neck. Yes, she came towards me. And I saw clearly . . . What was it? What was it in that moment? We spoke to each other, without . . . we didn't have to say the words, we read them in each other's eyes: "So we meet again. But we won't have the chance . . ."—that's what I read in her eyes— "won't have the gift of living together. It's now or never. These minutes may be all we have." Listen, Amy . . .' Moss was speaking directly to me, 'if anyone tells you this story, maybe it will be my friend here, who went looking for my manuscript with me, the manuscript I wrote for you . . .' Moss stared at me, his eyes never wavering from my face: 'But we didn't find it, Amy, not a trace. This friend of mine will tell you the story when I'm dead and gone. He'll tell you what happened that night, when I took her by the hand—

your mother. We went upstairs, where I'd asked for a room, we didn't say a word, we just clung to each other's hands. Not a word. And that night, Amy, I'm telling you, when no one thought we had a chance in hell, when we'd all given up, I saw her and she saw me. And I loved that woman, Amy, I loved her; he'll describe it for you, how all that matters is that moment when we drew you into life, and you were with us, conceived that night. We were all there together.'

By now it was completely dark. Moss and I were standing in the unlit alley behind the shops on Ventura Boulevard. We had long since given up the search. But Moss had dragged me along, drawing me deeper into his story with every word, holding me captive. He had spoken to me as if every word were testimony.

And now—I could see it as he finished speaking—they were standing before him, the woman and his daughter. He had them back. At this moment, in this moment of conception, Moss had gathered in all he had lost and found it complete. He had collected his life around him and said, 'You are both here. Nothing is missing.'

And nothing was missing.

And Moss glowed in the light of his visitation.

THREE

Rider on the Storm

At the end of January, a few months before war broke out in Iraq, we were sitting on the patio outside Starbucks and the old La Reina movie theater. Noah's, just a few steps down the street, was closed for renovation. I was with a group of Armenians who met there almost every evening. I had moved to a table off to one side because Ara, a filmmaker who had grown up in Beirut and in '75, during the civil war, had managed to escape to the US, was telling me a story from his childhood and I wanted to hear how it ended.

Ara was trying to retrieve his first movie experience—I no longer recall how we got onto this topic. At any rate, this experience was not as easy to remember as something like one's first kiss. As Ara began to describe his first film, the memory of an earlier film emerged, and from that another, and no sooner had he mentioned that one than fragments of a still earlier one rose to the surface, which he sensed he had seen 'at a time when I didn't distinguish between dream and reality'.

As the first raindrops began to fall and the rest of the group retreated into the cafe, we had taken refuge under the Starbucks umbrella next to Moby Disc. At that moment Gary came tearing around the corner. He hesitated for a moment upon recognizing me, cast a disdainful glance at the Armenian and broke into our conversation.

'I've got to talk to you, man.'

I waved him off. Gary had moved into Rex's old apartment in the Starlite. Pete had introduced us.

I no longer recall what I said—something along the lines of 'Not right now. Wait for me in the cafe,' though it was obvious to me that Gary was very upset.

Actually, I saw at a glance that something must have gone awry between the fifty-five-year-old Gary and the young woman he had introduced to us the night before on this same spot. He had been quivering and awkward, blushing with pride now and then. You could tell immediately that there would be trouble between them. Some of the Armenians even started making bets on him while Gary was arguing with others about the war ready to break out.

At one point, Gary had stretched his left arm across the girl's knees and grasped the arm of her chair, as if, using his arm as a shield, he were guarding her with his life.

'Someone's raped your woman!' he exclaimed, 'before your very eyes . . .' and he reached for the chair arm, 'and you want peace? They've raped America and you want to let them get away with it!'

The girl gave a tense little smile and, to bridge over the embarrassing moment, slowly leaned far forward, over Gary's arm. It looked as if she were leaning out a window to catch his eye.

'Come on in, welcome!' she exclaimed, laughing at Gary.

The Armenians laughed, too. Vahe, the painter, was much taken with Gary's 'date', and handed her and Gary invitations to the party he was giving the next evening.

'My party—you must come!'

I left soon afterward.

Ara's friends had told me the next morning that after leaving with his girl, Gary had turned up again at the cafe that evening, shortly after midnight. Alone and crestfallen. Things got heated again at some point. Gary called Vahe, who had asked him several times for the girl's cell phone number, 'a fucking foreigner' who didn't belong here. But Vahe had kept his cool and had pushed a twenty-dollar bill, and then another, across the table for the phone number.

'I don't give a damn what happens in Iraq,' Gary shouted, and tossed a crumpled piece of paper with the number onto the table. He was quite drunk but had the presence of mind to pocket the money. 'Let's drop some nukes on them! We Americans could use more golf courses,' were the parting words quoted to me.

So this was the Gary who found us on the patio. I assumed he would wait for me in the cafe—or maybe not—and urged Ara to continue his story about those early encounters with film.

'In Bourj Hammoud, the Armenian quarter in East Beirut, there were lots of movie houses,' Ara continued. 'I remember the Kermanic, the Florida, the Royal, the Sevan, the Knar—that's Armenian for harp, also used as a pretty girl's name—and the Madonna. But I think I saw my first film in the Cinema Arax. Next to the Cinema Arax was the Falafel Arax, which still exists, by the way, but it's in Hollywood now. Falafel Arax, on the corner of Normandie and Santa Monica Boulevard—do you know it?

'No, I don't.'

'We should go some time. The food tastes just the way it did in the fifties. Well, my sisters and their girlfriends, who always munched on black watermelon seeds during the movie—every halfway grown-up person snacked on them, and at the end of the show the floor was littered with the shells—stuffed me with falafel during this particular film; you'll see why, and why I remember it. I was their "little pet", whom they had to feed the way the animals in the film were fed. It was one of those awful low-budget movies from Italy that we were inundated with at the time—swords and sandals, Romans versus Germanic tribes, Christians versus lions, and this one was about the ark, the Flood, God versus mankind. And Noah, I remember, had to feed his animals and probably didn't have enough fodder in his gloomy ark, so they went hungry, while I was being stuffed with falafel in the darkened theater. But at some point I lost my appetite. I also no longer heard my sisters' giggling. Something striking had happened on the screen. Ten minutes into the film a group of boys in front of us shouted several times, "Halla balash al film!" which meant essentially, "Now it's really starting!"' Ara paused. For a moment, I thought he must have been reminded of yet another film, from even longer ago.

'I have to tell this differently,' he said, 'because in my eyes, it wasn't a "low-budget" production, not even a film in the usual sense. What was it that had brought all these people together in this darkened place? And what made those boys, who'd been joking around with my sisters, suddenly face the screen and listen up?'

Again Ara paused for a moment.

'Now I know why this film didn't occur to me sooner when I was trying to recall my first movie experience. Later, I made my sisters tell me the story again and again, so often that I remembered it as a fairy tale, one with vivid images, but like the tales in the books my sisters read to me when they were putting me to bed at night. The film was about the ark, as I said. And Noah and his sons. He had three sons. But there was another.'

'Another son?'

'I don't think so. Or maybe he was. A prodigal son, perhaps. I don't recall. At any rate, his name was Ur. But the film began with Noah, the building of the ark, and then . . . the camera must have panned to the side, and there, in a thicket, behind felled cedars, it focused in on him. This Ur. It looked as if he were lying in wait. He was spying on Noah and his sons, watching them bring animals, select them and then drive them in pairs up the ramp and into the ark. Then Ur slipped away. And we followed him . . .' Ara raised his hands as if he were following Ur with his camera. 'So why do I remember this? I think Ur had huge muscles. He could easily have picked me up and carried me on his shoulders. Without setting me down suddenly, as my sisters did almost immediately. Now I accompanied Ur through the underbrush, through a forest and came to a hut where he lived with his wife.'

'Is your baby-story going to take long?' I heard Gary saying behind me. Gary, whose name meant 'the spear'. He had pulled a chair under the overhang between the cafe and the CD-shop, and was sitting there with hunched shoulders, smoking and nervously whipping his foot into the rain. 'You're talking heathen nonsense, falsifying the Bible. Noah didn't have a prodigal son.'

Ara refused to rise to the bait.

'This woman—I don't remember her name—Ur loved her,' Ara continued. 'You could tell, because while she was cooking, he came to her, crouched by the open fire and gently encircled her ankle with one hand while with the other he covered his troubled face, making it look if he were just shielding it from the heat of the fire. My eldest sister, who couldn't read the Arabic subtitles but could follow the French ones, said, "He wants to save himself and his wife from the Flood, but by now Noah is letting only animals onto the boat, so it's too late for the couple."

'When his wife had fallen asleep—Ur was too troubled to sleep—he slipped out, checked the water in the well, searched the night sky for stars but saw none, then put his ear to the ground, as if trying to hear what was happening beneath the surface. Then he made his way to the river bank, having heard that a sorcerer spoke there at night with the animals. Once he arrived at the river, he came upon people who were feasting and dancing, wedding guests, as he could see, while an army of cooks and servants bustled around, slaughtering and roasting the animals and serving the bridal pair and their guests. One of the servants catches him by the goat pen, behind which he has crouched to watch the goings-on, and drags him in front of the cooks, who report him to the masters. The bride and groom, it seems, want to see who's messing around with the cooks' goats. And he is dragged by the hair through the laughing throng to face the couple. They question him and when he begins to speak, his fear of the Flood and the annihilation that will soon befall all those who didn't find a place in the ark seems to communicate itself to other guests. In the ensuing agitation, Ur implores the sorcerer, who is supposed to be somewhere in the crowd, to have pity on him. He looks around pleadingly and asks that he and his beloved wife be transformed into animals so they can be let into Noah's ark. At that, the bridegroom rises from his seat, throws off his bridal cloak, and Ur sees the pinions of an angel. "If it comes, this Flood," the angel addresses him, "it will destroy everyone—me, my bride, my guests and servants, you, your wife and—this much is certain—all those who have taken refuge in the ark. Do you not know," he says, "that the divine waters that are coming contain fire so hot that everything they surround will be consumed, this ark like kindling. And the pitch with which Noah is sealing the cracks will melt like wax in a flame and even the ashes of the ark will glow so hot that they will be driven through the water like a storm, blazing from the abyss with black sparks. Therefore, Ur, live!" exclaimed the angel. "Transcend your fear!"

'But Ur repeats his plea: "Turn us into two animals, that we may mount the ramp in time and find refuge in the ark."

'The angel beckoned to a servant. And Ur heard an animal being led up behind him and heard the snorting of a horse. When he turned around, the angel seized hold of him and lifted him onto the animal's back—it was a large goat-antelope with three long, black, twisted horns. Suddenly the ground disappeared under the animal. Ur saw no more sand beneath him and in the depths above which the animal's hooves hovered: nothing but stars—the night sky, which he had thought was above his head. And he threw his head back—around him only the starry night. Nothing else, no one else. And what lay before him—night and, far off in the distance, a glowing mist of stars—was divided in four by the animal's long horns. Fearfully he grasped the goat's pelt as the animal began to move. When he touched it, courage surged through him so powerfully that as the goat trotted out into the universe he fainted and tumbled off.

'In the gray light of dawn, he awakened in the rain. No trace of the ghostly company, as if he had dreamed it all. The river was rising rapidly. Ur hurried home, where he found that his wife was gone. The cottage stood empty. The bed where his wife had lain asleep only hours before looked trampled. He saw the tracks of an animal—a goat—on the floor, leading out of the house, towards the forest, in the direction of the ark, he thinks. Then the trail is washed away by the rain. Everywhere the ground is opening up but instead of being absorbed, the waters are bubbling out of the fissures. As Ur tries to make his way through the forest, he meets groups of people also trying to reach the ark. Suddenly, they hear a mighty roar behind them and an enormous wave rushes through the forest, pulling down trees and sweeping them all away.

'Now,' Ara continued, 'the image on the screen resembled what I saw on Saturdays when I was bathed in the tub and opened my eyes under water, while my sisters' hands reached in to hold me. At first you saw only what Ur saw. And then you saw him being buffeted by the current, struggling to get his head above water and being forced down time and again by steaming boulders and knots of human beings, from which he could free himself only with the greatest difficulty. He almost lost consciousness. But there was also fire burning underwater—they had simply superimposed glowing embers over the shot, very primitive, but effective: the water was on fire, consuming everything in it. And you saw Ur's face, contorted with pain, and his tunic appeared to be burning around his hips while his arms flailed above his head but couldn't reach the surface. Then blackness appeared before his eyes, as if everything were going dark, but what looked like a huge boulder rushed towards him. A moment later, he was clinging to it and being swept along. You saw Ur spread-eagled, hanging on with both hands as if onto the body of a whale, his hands digging into the whale's black hide. Eventually, you realized that it was no whale but the ark itself. Ur was clinging to the side of the ark, which was being catapulted through the water, swept under, then hurtled to the surface. And once the ark righted itself and was floating on the water again, you saw, through a dense curtain of rain, that Ur had jammed his hands and feet into the thick pitch with which the gaps between the hewn logs had been sealed and was thus held tight by the ark, like someone crucified with his face to the cross. And you saw that from the sea, on whose waves the ark was drifting, smoke rose up the ark's wooden sides, searing them with blazing spray. In places they were already on fire and the pitch with which they were sealed was dripping like wax from the cracks. Now you saw a scene inside the ark. Utter chaos. Noah's sons were trying to put out the fire, and the animals were in a panic and could not be quieted. The wooden sides were groaning as the masses of water hit them. Where the pitch had melted completely, water was spewing through the gaps between the planks, throwing smoky flames into the animals' feed as the creatures roared and raved. The wooden structure seemed about to split apart. Then came a close-up of goats and antelopes in one of the stalls. They were struggling to get away from the exterior wall of the vessel because in several places boiling water was bursting through.

'But one animal was striving to reach that very spot, pushing the others out of the way. And in the film you knew, or sensed, that it was none other than Ur's enchanted beloved. And now a cross-section through the smoking wall of the ark became visible, showing both sides of the wall that separated Ur and the goat. You also knew, or sensed: it won't be long now. On the right, you saw the goat's head butting through the softened pitch and tar in the wall, or already breaking through. A hose-like tunnel had opened up. It was like those films in which you look through a mouse's burrow, the camera providing a cross-section from the best vantage point. As the goat's mouth ate its way through the wall, on the other side of the wall, clinging to the exterior of the ark, you saw Ur. The boat's side in front of him opened gradually, forming a peephole through which he could now see her and she him—one eye gazing into the other.

'I don't recall how the rest of the action was filmed but later my sisters recounted, when I made them tell me the story, that in the moment when the two caught sight of each other the fires that had broken out in the ark died down, as did the fires outside; the smoke in the rafters dissipated, as if this unflinching meeting of the eyes had surrounded the ark with a protective mantle that prevented the waters from doing any more harm. Here someone had been reunited with his transformed beloved, never to lose her.

'In the end, as you know,' Ara continued, 'the ark came to rest on Mount Ararat in Armenia. And when the waters had receded, the door of the ark was opened, the ramp was lowered and the animals were driven out. And Noah and his sons set about making offerings. One of the sons reached for the she-goat but it darted away and hid among the other animals, and Noah's son took another. And now you saw a wide shot, actually another cross-section. On the right you could see the animals leaving the ark, passing the burnt offering that Noah was tending as the sun rose. And on the left side of the ark, in its shadow, you caught sight of Ur. Drained of strength, he was sitting on the ground, leaning against the planks of the vessel. Then the she-goat came dashing around the bow—and now you saw her very close up—found the exhausted man and knelt beside him, first leaning over him, then laying her head on his chest. And Ur put his arms around her. As he held her, he opened his mouth, and from his mouth poured water, a mouthful that he hadn't swallowed, water that was still warm because it had been hot from the fiery waters of the flood. As Ur let the water flow onto her head, it dripped warm onto her pelt and over his hands as they held her, and suddenly the woman was lying in his arms, restored. And they looked at one another. You saw the two stand up, Ur and his wife, and you asked yourself whether they would forever go unrecognized as they set out, leaving the shadow of the ark for the bright horizon.'

Lightning flashed several times above Mulholland. It was raining harder now as I drove through the hills a little while later with Gary. Along Laurel Canyon flowed a rushing brook, its water blackish brown. Now and then the brook changed sides, usually in the curves. Where the hillside dropped off, the brook would fan out and you had to drive even more slowly to avoid falling rocks shearing off the walls of the canyon.

I could not stop thinking about the transformative mouthful of water that Ur had been saving. While Ara was telling the story, I was carried back to my childhood, when, tormented by dreams about the World War, I would take a last mouthful of water from the kitchen before going to bed. As if I needed it to keep me alive through the night. Not until I was falling asleep did I let it drain slowly down my throat. It enabled me to survive the hours of darkness—like a flood against which my mouthful of water protected me.

Gary had managed to stick it out until Ara finished describing the film. Then he had dragged me along the front of the La Reina to show me his car, parked at the corner on Cedros Avenue. The police had immobilized it with a boot clamped to one of the front wheels. Gary had accumulated innumerable unpaid tickets, amounting by now to a large sum.

And if he could not redeem the car, which he needed urgently, especially today, it would be towed tomorrow. And the fines would be doubled.

'You know what it's like without a car in this city. Any chance I have of making a living . . .' he said, as if I were supposed to know what he meant by that.

He wanted my car. Just to borrow. I would have it back in the morning.

'Sorry, I need it myself,' I lied, 'tonight.'

Then Gary asked me to at least drive him to see some people in Laurel Canyon who owed him money.

'It's my only chance to get my car back. Do me the favor, man,' he said. 'We'll be there in no time. And on the way I'll show you the place where I lived in the sixties.'

'The sixties' and 'Laurel Canyon' were cues he slipped in because he had noticed that they made an impression on me. I had heard him talking a few times out by the pool—and had always followed up with questions—when he described his big years as a percussionist, a time when every wind gust in the canyon—always Laurel Canyon—was redolent of the marijuana that was smoked all night long in the houses the wind skimmed by. The next morning, as Gary told it, you would be awakened by the invisible flute-player who lived above the canyon and gently greeted the sunrise with 'Greensleeves'.

As soon as Pete introduced him to me, Gary countered with several stories, as if it were important for me to realize who I was dealing with. Still a percussionist, he had been the drummer for the Turtles back in the sixties.

'The Turtles?' I asked, knowing perfectly well who was meant. 'They were the ones who sang . . .'

Gary chimed in at once: ' "Happy Together". That was their greatest hit.' He began to sing, moving his hands as if he were casually beating the 4/4 time with his sticks:

Imagine me and you, I do
I think about you day and night,
It's only right
To think about the girl you love
And hold her tight
So happy together . . .

I asked him, as if I simply couldn't believe it, 'So you were the drummer on that record, "Happy Together"?'

In one way, my question was a compliment. Giving him a chance to repeat the information. In another way, it expressed my amazement that a song title I had not had occasion to mention in years now evoked images of unprecedented freshness, even though I had not really liked the song when it had come out. As if someone were showing me a photograph—from that time—in which I appeared, unfamiliar yet unmistakable. From a remote corner that had been illuminated by the name of that song, that period emerged as if it were today, present, sitting before me, so to speak, in the person of this man whom I had heard in those days wherever I went, when I entered a room with someone, to the beat of a song that this man—invisible—had drummed into the grooves, the canyons, of the record. Invisible and now visible, as if a photographer had been following me half my life, and had now revealed himself and shown me the photo—here, this is you.

But then came Gary's answer, which I had not thought to wait for. The answer that won me over to him because it set him apart from all those other people who would have dodged my question by simply not answering, or by responding with a nod to the question that was not a real question.

'No,' I heard Gary saying, 'that wasn't me. When they recorded "Happy Together", I'd already left the band.'

By the house, now in ruins, where Harry Houdini, the great magician and escape artist had once lived, we turned right, leaving Laurel Canyon for Lookout Mountain.

'That's the corner where Zappa lived, in a house that once belonged to Tom Mix, the star of silent Westerns,' Gary explained. 'And over there, we're about to come to it, is the house where Joni Mitchell wrote the songs for *Ladies of the Canyon*. Once a month, you'd line up in a little real-estate office next to the country store—that's farther down, the "store where the creatures meet"—and hand Mr. Mann a hundred-fifty bucks, the rent for the house. And the two guys in line in front of you, those were Mr. Nash and Mr. Crosby, of Crosby, Stills and Nash . . . Turn here.'

We turned off again.

'In the house over there . . . I lived with a woman for a while. Until one day I found John Mayall's moccasins under our bed.'

I laughed out loud as we drove past the modest bungalow and garage. Peering through the rain, I could easily picture, behind the house's small windows, the unmade bed with John Mayall's moccasins under it.

'And how could you tell . . .' I didn't finish the sentence. Gary struck the side window with his hand, as if he were annoyed at the way it kept fogging up. Now he said nothing for a while.

We turned left onto a small, fairly steep side street —Hermit's Glen, I read on the street sign—which ended after ten or twelve houses in a cul-de-sac.

'You turn the car around. I'll be back in a few minutes,' he said, got out of the car and ran, as I could see in my rearview mirror, back a few houses towards the entrance to a terracotta-colored house.

By the time I had turned and parked the car next to the flooded footpath, Gary had already disappeared inside. Or so I assumed.

What would he tell the people—who certainly would not be expecting him in this weather? By the garage, a ragged overgrown hedge marked the edge of the property. The branches were withered in one section and behind them I thought I glimpsed Gary for a second, or at any rate a man, silhouetted against the glowing turquoise oval of the swimming pool, who then disappeared again.

What was going on? Had that really been Gary? Maybe the owner, who, summoned by his wife, at this moment was looking at Gary in confusion: 'Gary here claims you owe him money.' No, Gary would have been more circumspect. At least I would have been, had I been in his position.

Several minutes passed. No sign of Gary. I switched off the engine.

The rain was pelting down so hard that I could barely see which of the houses along the street had lights on inside.

I thought of Ara's tale of the Flood, the jumble of images he had indubitably seen. I, too, had seen Ur before me and the little opening in the side of the boat that brought their eyes together. The way the eyes had locked onto each other. I recalled that as a child, as old as Ara when he saw the film, I had tried that with my dog. I had crawled up to him as he lay stretched out comfortably, had lain down on my stomach, positioning my face directly in front of him, then stared into his eyes. Deep into his eyes, without letting his go, without looking away. What did I want to know? I wanted to know whether he could really see me. Whether he was aware somehow that he was seeing. Seeing me. Also seeing into me, as I was seeing into him. And because I did not know but kept hoping that something inside the animal saw me, I sank way down, as if I were looking deep into the past. As if I had been that dog—as I imagined, no, as I knew at such moments. Yes, as if I still were—there, deep in his eyes—still an animal, untransformed.

Suddenly a shot rang out.

I was not mistaken. It was a shot. But from where? I thought it came from the house into which Gary had disappeared. Good God, was that possible? From one of the nearby houses at any rate. I tried to remain calm—maybe it was just a car backfiring or . . .

No, a shot.

I peered out the side window, and locked the passenger door. Better safe than sorry, I thought.

Where did the shot come from? From the right or left side of the street? Maybe it wasn't a shot after all. I forced myself to consider that possibility. From where? Since I could not answer the question with any certainty, I tried to calm myself: you don't even know where the sound came from. Or what it was. All you hear is rain, just rain. You don't hear any cars, any doors . . . any screams. And why should you?

Someone was trying to open the car door. I saw an arm tugging at the handle.

Gary. It was Gary.

I leaned over and opened it for him.

'Whoaaa . . . I'm soaked,' he said.

'And?'

'Everything's OK. Let's go.'

'Did they give you money?'

'No one was home. They're still away on vacation.'

'Hey, what's going on? Look at me, man,' I said.

'What should be going on?'

'You've been . . . You've been smoking something, man. Are you high?'

'So what if I am?' Gary replied, 'it's none of your . . .'

'You're high and you . . . Were you inside the house? Where were you?'

'What's eating you, man? Take it easy!'

'I want to know what's going on. I saw someone over there—was that you?'

I pointed past him to the hedge.

'No, man, no, I was . . .'

'Someone was there.'

'I think they're still on location.'

'Still on . . .? Who lives there?'

'Someone I know, real well,' Gary laughed.

'And the shot?'

'So?'

'You heard it?'

'I did. I did. Take it easy, man. Here I was feeling mellow and no sooner do I relax than you get all worked up. Come off it, man, come off it.'

'And where did the shot come from?'

'How should I know? In the canyon everything echoes.'

'In rain like this?'

'That . . . hey, how should I know? At least it sounded like a shot.'

'And where did the stuff come from?'

'What stuff?'

'The stuff you just smoked.'

Gary looked like someone trying to grin through acute pain.

'Little Kahuna, man. They have a hiding place out back on the patio. That's where I . . .'

'You weren't inside the house at all?'

He looked at me in astonishment.

' . . . took something for my pipe. On the patio. He owed me money, after all.'

'You deal?'

'Whoaaa, man . . . take it easy. I just . . . just took a quick look out back to see whether . . . Sometimes he sits on the patio with his old lady, having a smoke while they watch the Rain Channel. Good people, man. He always was a decent guy.'

'OK, Gary. We're heading back now.'

'He got me a role one time as a doctor on *ER*. Not that long ago. I was a doctor, man! I was an ER doctor. Total chaos . . . and me smack in the middle of it.'

He laughed, pounded himself on the chest, then looked down, as if his name tag were still there, the kind all the doctors on the show wore.

'Timothy L. Robert, MD: that was me—the extras' favorite doctor, I'm telling you. That made me the drug doc, "Dr. Robert". You remember the song?

"He's a man you must believe," McCartney sings. I had on real cool aquamarine scrubs. Sometimes you can see me going by in the background or I'm pointing out something on a patient's chart to one of the other doctors in the background or I'm discussing a fever curve with one of my colleagues . . . Man, those were the days! They paid well. And his assistant director, she always had the best weed. Maui waui . . . One morning I come breezing in and I'm about to put on my lab coat—Dr. Robert, ready to save the world—and they hand me blue overalls. "Hey, what's going on?" I ask. "You're going to change a bulb in the corridor." "OK, OK, electrician," I say, "I can do that." You get it? It's TV. But . . . Anyway, I do it. They're shooting, shooting in the hallway, and the doctors who earn the big bucks are hurrying past me: Noah Wyle, of course, and "Doug Ross", the doctor who saves kids' lives, my idol—George Clooney, I mean—with a couple of nurses in tow, they all hurry by, with the Steadicam in the lead. Suddenly I hear "Cut!" and "Hey, hey, what's going on here?" I hear one of them saying. I can still hear it. It was the director. The guy who used to live here . . .'

'So who lives here now?'

I saw I was confusing him and let him continue.

' . . . so he yells, "Cut!" Right after the Steadicam passes me with George and Noah. Cut, man! And then

119

I hear my name. He's yelling, "Gary! Gary! What are you doing there?" And I say—and I almost drop the bulb, I'm so . . . "Man!" I say, "I'm changing a bulb here, I . . ." And he yells, "Gary!" He interrupts me, right, doesn't let me finish. Interrupts me in front of all those people and says, with Clooney and Wyle standing right there, "Gary, Gary, you're a doctor. A doctor, Gary!" "But they told me . . ." "Forget the bulb! Forget the damned bulb! What the hell are you doing here, man? You're a doctor, Gary! Now get yourself over to costuming and suit up properly!" Wow . . . and that in front of all those people, the whole . . . I mean, there were other cast members in the background and the crew, of course . . . "You're a doctor, Gary!" And in that episode, man, I hit my all-time record—I appear twice! First, I'm climbing my ladder to change the bulb and then I'm dashing off with my stethoscope around my neck to confer with a colleague.'

I could not help laughing.

'What a life,' I said.

'And now. Now it's all over, you know?'

'How come?'

'It's all supposed to be over.'

I asked again, but received no answer. Suddenly he was silent and dejected.

'Can you . . .' he asked but didn't finish.

'Come on, I'll drive you back.'

I started up the car and headed for Laurel Canyon.

'I'm begging you,' he said suddenly, 'I'm begging you, man. Don't drive me back there, man. I've got to . . . I've got to see her again. It's all because of her. I have to go to her, have to explain . . .'

I pulled over.

'Either you tell me what this is about, or . . .'

'But I told you . . .'

'Gary, I like your stories. But you're trying to distract me. What's this really about?'

I could not get anything out of him. Not until I went to start the car again did he put his hand on my arm.

'I've made a colossal mistake, man. She has to forgive me.'

'What's wrong, Gary? Who do you mean?'

'Grace.'

This was the first time I had heard her name. Grace was the young woman he had been with at Starbucks the night before. He said he had met her that morning at the Starlite.

'She lives there?'

'She was sitting by the pool, dangling her legs in the water. "I'm waiting for Pete," she said. He'd gone to get the keys from June. Then we checked out the vacant studio apartment. She comes from Carmel, by the way.'

'And?'

'She's an actress . . .'

'Good God, Gary.'

'No, seriously. She wants to study acting and . . . well, move here. She had a couple of appointments lined up in the afternoon with agents, who . . . Anyway, I arranged to meet up with her in the evening. We went around the corner from Starbucks and were going to take my car. "We won't get very far with that," she said. That was when I noticed the boot. I was so embarrassed, but, I dunno, I think it was when I saw her looking all concerned, as if someone had really done me wrong. Suddenly, I was in a terrific mood. That surprised her. She was so sweet, you know. She said, "How are you going to get the car back? Where will you get the money?" As if this had happened to "us". As if she were asking, "What are we going to do?" She was so concerned, it was wonderful. And I thought to myself, "Will you look at that? Such a beautiful girl! You must admit, she's . . . admit it, she . . ."'

I shrugged: 'So what are you after?'

'I just want you to see it the same way. So you understand how I . . .'

'Well, what happened?'

'We grabbed something to eat at the place on the corner. And I noticed that she was catching my good mood. "What are you going to do?" she asked again. And that made me think . . . well, I told her about Jesus.'

'Good God, Gary.'

'Shut up! I had a right to do that. She'd touched me so much that I thought I had to tell her where I'm coming from . . .'

'She was the one who touched you, Gary. It was her! A young woman. And then you go and dredge up this "Jesus" stuff, man!'

'Isn't it right for her to know how things stand with me? I'm not afraid to show her. I said, "There's no secret to it, Grace. I can tell you who saved me. His name is Jesus. He died for my sins. That's something I didn't grasp for a long time."'

'Good God, she must have been wishing she could disappear in a puff of smoke.'

'"I hand my burden over to Him," I told her, "and all my troubles. He'll take them on. He's already taken them on! My Savior."'

'She listened to all that?'

'I could tell right away that she doesn't know Jesus.'

'How refreshing.'

'That she doesn't know Him, and . . .'

'So you know Him?'

'I told her about the small congregation I joined in the Valley, the Keepers of the Flame. She heard me out—not like you! Yes, she even asked, how I . . . how I found my faith.'

Gary sat there, looking down, as though he were sitting across from Grace again, and were quietly collecting himself to answer her question. As if the question were still before him.

I realized we were parked by one of the houses he'd pointed out to me earlier. John Mayall's dusty moccasins were lying by the ghostly bedpost, somewhere on the other side of the rain-curtained wall.

'I told her first . . . about my marriage, so she'd understand the desperation that drove me . . .'

'You're married?'

'Was, was. I married in '67 and five years later, we divorced. Everything went wrong. I was constantly off on tour with some band or other, only in L.A. now and then. And she—ran off with the Doors' drummer. Since that time I can't stand the Doors.'

'Riders on the Storm . . .' I sang. It was the Doors' song that begins in the rain. 'Into this house we're born . . .'

'. . . Into this world we're thrown,' Gary sang along, laughing, as though he saw those days before him.

'I met her in the parking lot outside the jail! She came on to me, that girl did. "Hey, don't I know you?" The night before our band had played in the Whisky. Whisky a Go-Go. Between two sets we get a call from our manager: "As soon as you're done there, come over to Curson Terrace, there's a party here. The Beatles want to meet you!" The Beatles, man! They were in L.A. for what would be the last time and were appearing in Dodger Stadium. So we went straight there from the set. Down Sunset, six of us in one car, up to Curson Terrace. The street ends in a cul-de-sac, up in the Hollywood Hills. And from a distance we can see—the whole area is packed with fans. The closer we come, the more insane the scene is. The crowd completely insane, swarming outside the houses and calling for the Beatles. And cops. Cops who stopped us: "You can't get through here. Turn around." "No, man," we say, "we were invited! Third house on the right—we have the number—let us through." "You're turning around," they shot back. We'd been smoking, were feeling no pain, and then something like this. The cop who leaned over and stuck his head in the car window—I don't think he knew what that strange smell was, but one of us said,

"Bummer." And the cop must have heard "Bum" and thought we were insulting him. "Out, all of you out!" We had to get out of the car and be searched. They searched the car, too, and found a couple of joints. Put us in handcuffs and took us away, with all those people looking on. They left the dome light on in the cop car so everyone could see in. The car crept at a snail's pace down Curson, past all the fans who were still making their way up the hill. On the way to the station, the cops smoked the joints. So we knew it wasn't going to be that bad. We spent the night in a cell, and the next morning . . . as I said, I saw the woman in the parking lot outside the police station. She said she'd seen me the day before outside the house where the Beatles were partying. She'd just been released herself. She'd climbed over the fence on Curson Terrace. Crawled into the house through an open bathroom window in the back. Then ran through all the rooms looking for John, Paul, Ringo and George. Crazy! It turned out she was in the wrong house. The guy who lived next door to the Beatles caught her and called the cops. Later she always claimed, in all serious-ness, that she was the one who inspired McCartney's song "She Came in Through the Bathroom Window".'

'And that's who you married?'

Gary nodded and said nothing for a while. 'Forty days of flood—that's what your Armenian buddy was describing. You know, sometimes I have the feeling I've been up to my neck in water for forty years. Always close to drowning. Never having firm ground under my feet . . . I'm fifty-five years old, man! And what do I have to show for it? Zilch.'

'What if you'd been able to get into the Beatles' mansion that day?'

'Ha! That would have been the party to end all parties. They tossed steaks over the gate to the fans outside, and pulled groupies in from the crowd. Our manager told us the next day what we . . .'

'No, I mean, what if you'd been let in, if they'd opened the gate and you'd gone inside. You'd never have met your wife.'

'If we . . .' Suddenly he laughed. 'You mean, if we'd gotten into the Beatles' ark. Jeez, I can't let myself think about it . . . My life would have turned out completely differently. Completely.'

He seemed so certain of that, so desperately certain that he narrowed his eyes to slits, as if he could read the warm trace of the very different life that had once awaited him inside that gate and, if he exerted himself to the utmost even today, might still be there for him. He rubbed his face as if he were just waking up.

'I can't even make it to first base anymore,' he said. 'I . . . mess everything up. I meet Grace . . . and the devil snatches away my salvation.'

'Salvation from what?'

He looked at me and hastily reached into his right jacket pocket. For a second I thought he was going to show me something. But he stopped himself, then stuck his other hand under his thigh, as if he were feeling cold.

'All I told Grace was that the marriage didn't work out. That everything went downhill. After it was over—we'd been divorced for a year by then, and I'd pretty much hit bottom—I started a relationship with another woman. Nothing special. Just for sex and drugs. A crutch, something to keep me above water. After three months, she told me she had to move to Chicago. For a job. Maybe she thought I'd move with her. But I didn't want to. Let her go, I thought. There was no love involved, after all. We arranged to meet one last time, coming from different directions, in a motel in Carmel.'

'Carmel? And you told that to Grace, who . . .'

'. . . comes from Carmel, I know,' Gary replied. 'Yes, I told her. Because it was there . . . in Carmel, that the turning point came for me. It was the next day, when I was taking the Pacific Highway from Carmel back to L.A., and I was so depressed, really at rock bottom. Saying goodbye to this woman had somehow brought it all to the surface, the hash I'd made of my life. I was crying as I drove, thinking I couldn't possibly go on. And as I drove, the idea came to me—I could put an end to it all. You know the coastal road, how it winds along the cliffs. Every curve offers you a chance not to turn the wheel. Time and again. Time and again I was tempted . . . to let it all go. To step on the gas and go straight over the cliff into the ocean. And once I pointed the car in that direction. Now! I told myself. At that moment, as if someone were yelling at me, an image flashed before my eyes. I saw myself on my knees, praying. Tightened my grip on the steering wheel and turned it hard, away from the edge. I knew what I had to do. That was the beginning, the turning point. Jesus saved me. Grace listened to the whole story quietly. She understood, you know?'

'But?'

'She couldn't believe in such things, she said. That vision had to be a holdover from my childhood. My belief in Jesus . . . something I'd picked up. I'd never seen Jesus, never spoken to Him.'

'She's right.'

'She said the only thing she believed in was what she'd experienced herself. "Either you help yourself, or you go out like a light." One time she'd joined a group that was planning to hike up Mount Whitney. During the last third of the ascent, they'd been caught in a storm. None of them helped each other— it was every man for himself. During the storm, as she pressed herself against a cliff that offered meager protection, she realized there was no one, no God. The wind swept some of the party away, pulled them off the mountainside. "Without rhyme or reason. Cold, completely indifferent." Those people were swept away silently, in the darkness. No one saw anything. Only later did it become clear what had happened. She herself managed to cling to the cliff only with the greatest difficulty, and, "just like you," she said, in her exhaustion, she kept coming to the point where it seemed reasonable simply to let go. When she said "just like you," I realized how profoundly she understood me.'

'I hope you didn't try to convince her that those ideas came from the devil, and that Jesus . . .'

'No, no, I controlled myself. I was still . . . I was still under the spell of that "just like you." And then she . . . she had a chain around her neck, which she pulled out from under her blouse. On the chain was a tarnished silver locket. She said she had this chain on during the storm. And when the storm threw her down and she tried to reach for a boulder, this chain tumbled out of her clothing and the wind whipped it against her cheek. She tapped two or three times on a spot below her cheekbone. "The locket struck me pretty hard," she said. "It reminded me that there were people waiting for me at home." She reached around her neck, unfastened the chain and opened the locket. Inside, I saw a couple of stiff black curls resting in cotton wool, with black dust around them. I had no idea what they were. She quickly snapped the locket shut. "I don't usually show this to people," she said.'

'And what was it?'

"'My mother's and my grandfather's voice," Grace said. They were bits of an old phonograph record. Grace had come upon a whole box of records in the attic and her mother had told her that her grandfather had sometimes sung into an old device, an antique, whose stylus engraved the sounds directly into a record. In those days, you had one original, no copies. As the stylus dug into the disk, thin black spirals of shellac curled out of the grooves, which her mother was allowed to remove with an old toothbrush while the recording was being made, to keep them from blocking the stylus. Sometimes her father had his daughter sing along and then explained to her—because he didn't want to entrust the records to the child—that the "black curls" were the other impression of their voices. The curls matched the grooves exactly. If you placed them on top of the grooves, the two would fit together like clasped hands, and there would be nothing left over.'

Gary paused for a moment. Again he struck the window with the back of his hand.

'Hey!' I exclaimed.

'I'm going to crack this window,' Gary said nervously. 'I need a smoke.'

He lit a cigarette and rolled down the window. As the sound of the rain rushed in, he puffed hastily and continued to talk.

'Why I . . . completely nuts! I must have been nuts to . . .'

'In love.'

'No . . . I mean, yes, certainly in love. But because she was sharing these things with me, I . . . fool that I was, I thought I could tell her everything. Had to tell her everything. Make a fresh start with her. So I admitted that earlier I . . . hadn't been totally honest. Hadn't told her the whole truth. But now I wanted to do that, since . . . every Keeper of the Flame has to begin with the truth, which is Jesus. "I feel I must make a fresh start," I said. "Have to. With you."'

'So how did she react?'

'Well, I was looking down. I was embarrassed ... But the devil, it was the devil, I tell you, made me keep talking. I told her what I'd never admitted to anyone.'

He fell silent for a while, then tossed his cigarette out of the car but did not close the window.

'That time in Carmel, when the woman and I saw each other for the last time, she didn't want to have sex. She didn't want to smoke. She was sad that it was all over. She wanted to talk. I didn't believe her.'

'Believe what?'

'So I ... forced myself on her.'

'Forced yourself?'

'Raped her,' Gary said.

No sooner had he spoken the word than he realized it would turn Grace against him. In the grain of the restaurant tabletop, which he was staring at because he did not have the courage to look up, he saw a glowing eye. In dizzying succession, one image after the other welled up out of the darkness—the wrinkles and folds in the sheet under which the woman had tried to take refuge, the vertigo that seized hold of him as he drove towards the cliff, the steering wheel whipping around, the stylus biting into the shellac. When he looked up, Grace had averted her eyes. She rose from the table, her face drained of color, and walked away.

We sat silently in the car for a while. Then I asked him what he hoped would happen if he saw Grace again. My own thinking, I said, was that she would never be able to forgive him.

'Gary, the woman you should be seeking out lives in Chicago, or . . .'

'You don't know that,' he interrupted me. 'You don't know whether Grace can forgive me. Grace wouldn't know herself. That will be decided—and not by her, not by me—only when she looks me in the eye.'

He sensed that I would remain adamant and was still focused only on how I could extricate myself from this situation as quickly as possible.

'It's the one thing I still want, man. A chance to see her. Tomorrow . . . no, today even, you'll be rid of me.'

He tapped me on the shoulder.

'Come on.'

I started the car and drove by way of Lookout Mountain to the ridge, then followed his directions to Appian Way. At Sunset Plaza, we turned and started downhill. Here the mist was clinging so densely to the hillside that we had to creep along. Now and then, on the right, on the brink of the precipice, palms reared up between bungalows. People had strung lights on them. On the left side of the road there were castle-like mounds, their sides coated in concrete, designed to protect the properties against landslides. One time a car coming in the opposite direction braked only a few yards from mine. For several seconds we faced each other, the danger forgotten, and were amazed at the image our headlights captured—rain coming down so hard that it seemed to hover above the asphalt in a glowing layer, as white as snow.

'There...'

After the next curve in the road Gary pointed to a line of cars parked along the side of the road. At the top of a steep driveway, a portion of a brightly lit house could be seen and, crowded in front of it, the rain-glistening cars of party guests, some of whom were wending their way towards the entrance, holding umbrellas or coats over their heads.

'You know what I was afraid of yesterday?' Gary asked, as I stopped at the bottom of the drive to let him get out. 'I had no idea I was going to tell Grace about

Carmel. But I was afraid, terribly afraid that she might ask me whether I had children. "Do you have children, Gary?"—a perfectly innocent question. I'd mentioned my marriage, she'd talked about her mother and her grandfather. I was thinking, any minute now she's going to ask, "Do you have children?"'

'And why . . .'

He interrupted me. 'She's hardly older than my son was at the time. One night he dashed across the street, he told me later, because he'd recognized a couple of guys standing outside a gas station. Went up to them. And one of them handed him a gun, pressed it into his hand, as if it were a joke. And no sooner did he have it in his hand than he saw the gas-station owner inside the shop. Shot, sprawled on the floor. My boy got arrested. The others lie, fingering him as the shooter. I'd not spent . . . I hardly knew him, see. Frank had always lived with his mother but it was me he came to. That was my chance. He came to me, needed my help. He was innocent and he was placing all his hopes in me. I could have found him a good lawyer who would have gotten him off. But I needed every frigging penny for drugs, for rent, for . . . I kept putting it off till I was sure—sure that as far as he was concerned, I was dead.'

Abruptly Gary got out of the car. I leaned across the passenger seat to hold the door open as if I had an answer for him, something more to say. But he moved towards the house without turning around. In that fraction of a second, I saw something that increased my uneasiness even more. I had the distinct impression that Gary's right hand, which he had stuck into his jacket pocket as soon as he started walking, had closed around a weapon in that pocket. Impossible to actually see that. In my mind it was the gun that had been handed to his son and that had appeared vividly before me seconds earlier. What had I really seen?

Then I remembered the shot, the shot I had heard while I was sitting in front of the house waiting for Gary. Gary had heard it, too.

I got out of the car and hurried up the drive. But Gary had already disappeared into the house.

In the crowd of partygoers, I could not make him out at first. Hundreds of guests filled two entire floors. In the enormous living room, people were dancing. I pushed my way through, staying close to the wall, and reached a wall of glass, beyond which I could see the yard, with an illuminated swimming pool farther back on the right, also tennis courts. Several people were in the pool, frolicking in the rain. Not far from there, closer to the middle of the yard, others were warming themselves by a fire pit under the roof of a gazebo with spear-tipped railings.

As I looked around, I spotted Ara nearby and made my way over to him. He had not seen Gary and, in the racket, it was hard to explain why I was looking for him. But then I recognized Vahe near the top of the staircase that led to the floor above. I also thought I saw Grace, with whom Vahe was slowly descending the stairs, stopping repeatedly to talk to other guests. I forced my way through the crowd, again staying close to the wall, and waited at the foot of the staircase until they finally reached the spot.

Vahe seemed astonished to see me there and became annoyed when I tried to pull Grace, who did not recognize me, aside to talk to her.

At that moment screams became audible through the din. Several people pushed past us and I saw that the crowd in the living room was parting, stamping away from the glass wall as if fire had broken out there. A shot rang out and again we heard screams. I thought I saw dust drifting down from the ceiling. Some people immediately crumpled to the floor, while others rushed to the door, from which cries were also heard. I backed away, crouched behind the newel post and saw—on the other side of the room—Gary. His face distorted and with tears streaming down his cheeks, he pressed the gun to his temple and advanced a few steps towards someone who had fallen. It was one of the Armenians from the group that gathered around Vahe.

Gary shouted something at him, inaudible through all the noise. Yet I thought I knew what he had shouted:

'Where is she? Where's the one I'm looking for?'

He towered over the trembling man who was trying to answer. The Armenian pointed—I saw his finger touch the glass—through the pane to the outside.

Gary climbed over him to a sliding door, pushed it open and stepped out. At that moment, someone stopped the music and the voices fell silent. Next to me, a few people were making calls on their cell phones.

I do not know whether Vahe and Grace were in another group—I glimpsed Ara among them—who cautiously approached the glass wall, obviously intent on seeing whether the madman would shoot himself outdoors.

Some people were shouting that the police had been called. Then someone responded scornfully, 'Idiots. He'll take care of it himself.'

I made my way past the group, which was blocking the sliding door, to one of the side entrances, dashed outside, keeping close to the house, and into the yard to the left of the roofed patio immediately outside the glass wall.

Gary was standing in the rain, halfway to the pool. He had the weapon in his hand but no longer pointed at himself.

He hesitated, then went over to the seven or eight people bobbing in the water, who were unaware of the panic that had broken out in the house. For a moment it looked as though he thought Grace might be among them. Then he stopped again, looking up into the pouring rain.

A couple who had hoisted themselves out of the pool and moved onto the grass laughed as they pushed their way through the billows of steam that surrounded them. They began to chase each other, shouting as they ran past Gary, paying no attention to him.

I called out to Gary. Other shouts could be heard, directed at the couple.

Gary seemed not to notice but stood there.

The couple gamboling on the lawn did not understand why people were calling to them. They ignored the interruption and continued to chase each other, past me and back towards the pool. Shortly before they reached the edge of the pool, the woman looked behind her and stumbled. But she immediately righted herself on her knees and pointed to something diagonally behind me.

I turned and saw two policemen, guns at the ready, who were advancing cautiously, step by step, towards Gary from different directions. One of them noticed me and indicated to me with a gesture that I should get down on the ground. Then he called through the rain to Gary, ordering him to drop his weapon.

Gary . . . I had stopped in my tracks but was not yet on the ground . . . was Gary about to turn around? I could not quite tell. He did not drop his weapon.

Nor did he turn to face the policemen behind him. He was staring straight ahead at the fire burning a few steps away in the gazebo.

The policeman called out to him again. Now Gary was moving, it seemed to me, towards the fire.

I heard a shot—a warning shot.

And saw that Gary, still holding the gun, turned partly around as he walked, as if he had heard someone coming up behind him.

Then another shot rang out. Gary's shoulder jerked forward. The weapon fell from his hand, apparently without his noticing.

He stumbled, struggling to stay upright, and collapsed near the fire. As he fell, I could clearly see that he was reaching with his arms, maybe trying to break his fall. He toppled over in this position, both arms vanishing into the flames.

His body writhed, was shaken, but he held on tightly to something—or was held. At any rate, he did not pull his arms out of the fire. I could not tell what was happening until I jumped up and reached the fire pit at the same time as one of the policemen who, together with me, tried to drag the man by his legs out of the fire as he attempted again and again to prop himself up on his burning arms, as if he were locked onto something in the fire.

As we tugged at him, two blazing logs broke free of the fire, Gary's trembling hands still holding onto them, his fingers clawing them, as if digging into snow. It was Ur I saw and recognized immediately, Ur holding onto the burning ark, seeking the spot behind which his soul was waiting to be transformed once more.

FOUR

The Woman in the Sea of Stars

Pete's voice reached me as if through a dense fog. Now and then I closed my eyes, which were still burning. How much I had missed during the last few days, and again today! Pete was filling me in, convinced that the spoonfuls of hot soup from Noah's, together with his usual gossip, would have a restorative effect and get me back on my feet.

'Just think,' Pete said, 'since this morning, June's had company. Her "first relative to come by in a quarter-century". And June's not exaggerating. No one's ever turned up looking for her. No one knows about the bridal gowns she's been buying on sale for years and keeping for someone, God only knows who, some "nieces" she refers to. And this morning someone called Jennifer walks into the Starlite, rings June's bell, and sure enough—June and Jennifer are related. June claims she recognized her niece immediately by her beautiful red hair, which June supposedly brushed when Jennifer was little. You should have seen June. I'd stopped by to put the cheese cake

I'd just bought for her at Marie Callender's in her ice-box when the bell rings, June opens the door and promptly drops the porcelain vase . . . not a cheap one, either . . . And I—well, she introduced me to her Jennifer, but then I had to sweep up the pieces while the two of them sat on the couch and began to talk non-stop. I gathered that Jennifer—who recently got divorced, by the way; her young son spends the weekends with his father—has been living in Pasadena for over thirty years. Not even fifteen miles away! June's birthday is tomorrow, her seventy-seventh, and she immediately invited Jennifer to spend the night. I'm afraid that once June's had a few, she'll want to show Jennifer all the bridal gowns. That'll be something to see,' Pete added, and bent towards me and whispered, 'Who knows, maybe one of them fits Jennifer.'

I had followed only half of Pete's flood of details. I was having enough trouble getting down the matzo-ball soup he had fetched from Noah's and brought to my sickbed. Now Pete launched into speculation about the exotic herbs and other ingredients Luz had put in just for me. But also about what it could mean that Luz had refused to charge him—and that meant me—a single penny for the soup.

'I'm thinking you could be in line to become Rex's successor at Noah's. What do you say?'

'What time is it?' I asked weakly.

'Noon.'

Pete saw that this information made little impression on me. '*Saturday* noon. And the temperature out in the courtyard is almost as high as yours. June says if your fever doesn't break by tomorrow I should get you to the doctor's.'

From outside I heard the splash of someone diving into the pool. On hot days it was not unusual to see June, slim in her black one-piece suit, swimming in the Starlite Terrace's pool. Her skin was deeply tanned, her blond hair stuffed into an old-fashioned bathing cap. She swam even at night, diving into the brightly lit water.

I knew little about June. Only that the monthly rent check had to be dropped off with her. Pushed through the mail slot, including at those times when she was down by the pool. June was the Starlite's manager. 'Used to be an executive secretary at Fox,' Pete had mentioned once. 'Her family's originally from Prussia,' he'd added, as if to suggest that she and I were related somehow, or at least to excuse the authoritarian tone in which June directed Pete to attend to some janitorial tasks—for cash or reduced rent, I assumed.

When I had obediently slurped down Luz's matzo-ball soup and Pete had left, I lurched to the door and locked it behind him. No more visitors today. All I wanted to do was sleep.

Nonetheless, as I was standing by the door, I briefly parted the louvres of the blinds, blinking in the light, because I'd heard voices outside.

June was nowhere to be seen. Pete was standing by the pool. He called to a woman who was swimming laps and she responded to him. June's niece, I thought. What was her name again? Jennifer. Pete pointed to the sky, laughed and then headed upstairs energetically, taking two steps at a time.

Pete—'energetically . . . two steps at a time'? Was I seeing right? Or was I asleep and dreaming on my feet?

As I was about to let go of the blind, the woman pulled herself out of the pool to dry out on the warm flagstones. By the edge of the pool lay a black book, open, in which she wrote something.

A diary, I thought. Or is she drawing? I was pleased to see that unlike June—relative or not—she was not out there just to work on her tan. No, she was drawing . . . drawing something that was hanging under the beach umbrella; I heard the fabric rustling in the breeze. It was one of June's can't-beat-the-price bridal gowns. The ones Pete had referred to. It billowed like a wind sock, demandingly, its hem fluttering from the shade into the light. I saw the flash of a silver safety pin, from which dangled the pink sale-price tag.

'What are you drawing?' I asked Jennifer. I was back in bed, once more in the grip of a dream.

The woman pushed her red hair, still damp, out of her face and looked up at me. She gazed at me for a long time. Then she decided I was trustworthy.

'What do you see?' Jennifer asked and held out her black-bound book to me.

I studied the drawing, which she had placed inside a preexisting square, such as a storyboard artist uses when planning out sequences in a film. On this miniature screen she had made marks resembling a sickle moon, covered by fine hatching.

'I see hoof prints in the rain,' I replied firmly.

She seemed reassured and went back to her work. The stippling of the lines under her bent hand took on the sound of falling rain. Rain coming down hard and steadily, on a slant, her rain.

She looked up at me again, holding out the book.

'What do you see now?'

I saw that the rain was threatening to wash away the hoof prints. Soon every trace of a trace would be gone.

'We're going to lose them,' I told her.

She nodded with satisfaction—which alarmed me—and continued drawing.

In a corner of the book that had previously been covered by her wrist, I saw four marks in a square:

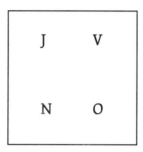

Finally, after what seemed like a long time, she asked again: 'What do you see?'

She held the book out to me, revealing the entire drawing.

At that moment, my fever broke. It broke at the sight of the page, which was a page no longer.

Instead, I was looking at a vast section of the universe. Colorful galaxies and glowing nebulae, huge clusters and spirals swirled in infinite expanses that my eye struggled to take in. I realized that what I was seeing had an order to it. From the red mane-mists and blue spiral galaxies of an eye—an eye staring straight at me—all the way to the glowing clouds of the nostrils, light years away, and the orange-blazing hollows of the panting mouth, I could piece together the sun-veined outlines of a horse's head, exploding into the universe.

Still in my dream, mastering this overwhelming composition suffused me with happiness. I felt as if I had long struggled to achieve this kind of all-encompassing view and now the power of my own eye to take it in had triumphed. What I had grasped had told me its name.

'Horse!' I said aloud in my dream.

And upon speaking the name, I awoke.

It was two hours before midnight when I got up, show-ered and dressed. The heat had waned only a little.

As I stepped outside, I heard June saying, during a lull in swelling film music, 'Him I knew personally!'

As she refilled her niece's glass with champagne, she pointed to the screen of her transistor television set, which she had placed on the table under the beach umbrella. Both women had terrycloth bath-robes draped over their shoulders, as if they had just climbed out of the pool. Galloping hooves could be heard. I squinted at the credits scrolling on the screen . . .

Music by
Victor Young

The film composer was just sending a horde of horsemen, accompanied by a full orchestra.

Print by
Technicolor

It was a rather scratched print. The live show taking place at poolside seemed more entertaining— June's and Jennifer's gestures with the champagne bottle and the glasses, and with the terry robes that kept slipping off their shoulders. With Victor Young's stirring martial music as a background, the women seemed comically dashing. 'Wild carousing by the pool,' the music suggested, 'dissolute women . . . Amazons . . . laying siege to the soft-spoken man.'

The moment they caught sight of me, June cheerily waved me over. 'Send him this way! He's seen us! Let's rend him limb from limb!' Young's rhythms thundered as she introduced her relative to me.

Jennifer was wearing a necklace of cowrie shells that June had given her and wanted me to admire. I liked it, liked it a lot.

Victor Young's witches' cauldron continued to boil as if the three of us were meeting in the midst of a storm, here by the water, to prophesy the future.

'Jennifer is a storyboard artist,' June told me.

The storm seemed to be subsiding, and behind me Young was introducing a peaceful, idyllic mood with strings and harp glissandos.

Jennifer smiled at my astonished expression. I was reminded of my dream, in which I had read correctly the traces she was drawing.

'Right now she's working on a project for New Regency,' June added when I failed to respond.

I was thinking that, at noon, Pete must have mentioned the storyboards. How else could I have dreamed it?

In my embarrassment, I glanced behind me at the television screen, where the noise was starting again. I saw clouds of red dust and, in their midst, a horse whinnying as it reared up . . .

'And Johnny Depp is interested in her!' June explained, as if I were not paying close enough attention.

Jennifer laughed.

'In the screenplay, June, not in me,' Jennifer corrected her.

'It can still happen,' June remarked, 'it's not too late.' And to me, 'Go get yourself a chair and join us.' June poured champagne into a water glass and turned to the television again.

'Now *that* was a man,' she said, more to Jennifer than to me.

Genghis Khan was wearing a ridiculous costume, but it was John Wayne. Unmistakable. And his booty, in a white robe, was Susan Hayward. Wayne was staring at her and any minute now would rip the white linen off her, just like that. Years ago, I had managed to sit through the first twenty minutes of *The Conqueror*. Later, I knew, Wayne would ride up to his mother's tent with his Tartar woman. And from then on, Agnes Moorehead, the mother, would have a premonition that things could only end badly—Wayne and Hayward in one tent. The gazelle Wayne had killed with a spear and ordered to be deposited at his mother's feet would not change that.

'We were renting office space from him back then,' June commented as we watched the images on the screen. 'And every morning, the first thing John Wayne would say to me was, "Where's the coffee?"'

June laughed and looked expectantly at Wayne, who had stormed into Hayward's tent, as if any moment he might ask about June's coffee again.

'This film was the death of him,' she said, 'which no one knew at the time. The idiots! They didn't —there, you'll see it in a moment—there, that red sand they're riding around in. You see it? It was all contaminated. They shot the film in the mid-fifties near St. George. A year before that, my girlfriend Betty and I went to Las Vegas—I've gone every year since '47, when I was twenty-one, old enough to gamble for the first time.'

'I wouldn't have thought you were . . .'

Hearing my compliment coming, June set down her glass.

'I'm the same age as Marilyn Monroe . . . would be today. She was born in '26, on the first of June—just like me. That's the God's-honest truth. Jennifer here didn't believe it either. In a couple of hours, we're going to drink to my seventy-seventh,' she laughed, her eyes darting back to the television.

'Those poor people. They could all be here with us today,' she remarked.

'So what about Betty and you?' Jennifer wanted to know.

'About Betty and me . . .?'

'You were going to tell us about Las Vegas,' Jennifer replied.

'Oh, yes, I'll never forget that trip. Betty and I took the bus. We stayed at the Flamingo. It was always the Flamingo. For me, at least. See, that was Bugsy's hotel.'

'Bugsy?' Jennifer asked.

'Bugsy Siegel. Never heard of him? Meyer Lansky? Lucky Luciano! . . . Murder, Inc.? Bugsy was the West Coast Mafia boss. He came out to Hollywood in the mid-thirties. He was involved for a while with Jean Harlow. She was the one Marilyn Monroe modeled herself on, down to the smallest detail. Not just the platinum-blond hair. He's buried in the Beth Olam Mausoleum over there in the Hollywood cemetery. That means "House in Paradise", someone told me. It's very nice. I wouldn't mind having something like . . .'

'Wait a sec, June—who's buried there?' Jennifer broke in.

'Bugsy, Bugsy Siegel, in the "Paradise". And it backs up on the Paramount lot on Gower Avenue. But that piece of real estate didn't belong to Paramount at the time. Not yet. In those days it was RKO. RKO Studios. That's where Fred Astaire and Gary Cooper made their films. So the RKO studio was located on land that was once part of the Hollywood cemetery. The same cemetery where Bugsy Siegel's buried. And then in the twenties, when films were already being made there, it belonged to Joe Kennedy, that same property. And Kennedy's father had a cozy relation-ship with the Mafia. Yes, siree. When the campaign got under way in 1960, he used that relationship to help his son, JFK. And how! By the way, the funny thing is that the orphanage where Marilyn grew up was just one street over, one street from RKO. It was an ugly red-brick building, torn down ages ago, but at the time it was still standing . . . on El Centro . . .'

June looked at us as if we could complete her thoughts at will. I was tempted to mention that Artie Ramirez had sold me my first car, a VW Beetle—and with it the key to this city—on El Centro, but I refrained.

'What a name!' June exclaimed. 'El Centro Avenue . . . But maybe it really is . . . and where it starts you're still like . . . in the middle, I mean, in the center. And from there everything seems visible. All still possible. And you see far into the future . . . but don't realize what you're seeing. They say Marilyn gazed longingly out her third-floor window every night, that orphanage window on El Centro, looking across at the illuminated ball. The RKO ball, I mean, the globe over by the corner of Gower and Melrose. It's still there. In those days, the RKO ball was always lit up at night. Little Marilyn hitched her dream to that ball as she looked out her window, into the light—her dream of being a movie star. Like Jean Harlow. Marilyn's Aunt Grace worked for RKO, you know. So you could say Marilyn already had one foot in the door, in the glow of the studios. But actually, I tell myself, if she'd known . . . she could have seen what was coming. She looked across there every night. If you think of it, she was actually looking at a graveyard. The graveyard where the studio was located, the studio that once belonged to the man whose sons . . . well, I'm sure you've heard that Bobby and Jack Kennedy were at least partially responsible for Marilyn's death. That May, Marilyn had sung "Happy Birthday" to her president. In that skimpy dress, skin-tight and covered with glitter, that left her back bare, she sang "Happy Birthday, Mr. President." At that time they were all still alive. Kennedy and Bobby and Marilyn. She'd just started working on her last film. The one for Fox that was never finished, in which she swam naked in a pool, and at the beginning of the film everyone thinks she's fallen out of the boat and drowned in the ocean. Three months later, she was dead for real. You've seen the photos of her last bedroom on Helena Drive . . . Supposedly they got rid of the crumpled note in her hand—"to avoid a scandal," I was told. It had Kennedy's phone number on it. Yes, siree. And Gable gave her her last kiss, her very last. Harlow also died young, at twenty-six, and Gable was the last one to kiss her, too . . . But . . . but what got me started on Marilyn?'

Jennifer came to her rescue. 'First you were going to tell us about Vegas and . . .'

'Right, about the Flamingo. And you didn't know who Bugsy was, Bugsy Siegel. Well, he certainly wasn't "the first man on the Las Vegas Strip", as they always claim. He lived with Virginia Hill. Never heard of her either? Hill was the great love of several of the "hoods" in those days—the scarlet woman, they called her. But Bugsy had fallen for her, hard. She owned a grand house in Beverly Hills. Not far from Beverly Hills High School. You take Beverly Glen to Sunset, turn left, and keep going till you come to Whittier. Then you turn right, drive a short stretch, till you see Linden Drive on your left, and it's right there, a mansion with two balconies under arcades. That was Virginia Hill's house. Bugsy had just had a manicure and was sitting in the living room on Virginia's couch. It was evening in Beverly Hills. Virginia wasn't there at the time. She was in Paris, I believe, shopping. Because Bugsy had beaten her up again. The machine gun shots came through a window on the side of the house. Hit Bugsy in the face. Tore it all up. That was in '47. As I said, a few weeks after my twenty-first birthday, when I was allowed to gamble for the first time in the Flamingo's casino.

'And Bugsy Siegel . . . did you see him there?'

'Oh, no. Bugsy always kept out of sight. Like Howard Hughes.'

'And Virginia Hill?'

'Didn't see her either. Virginia was always . . . well, she always happened to be elsewhere.'

As June was telling the story, she had mimed Bugsy Siegel's position on the couch when the bullets struck. Now she straightened up, stifled her laughter and acted as though she were hunting around for Virginia Hill. Then she was Hill herself, living it up in Paris, and handing me her glass for more champagne. Miss Hill drained her glass at one gulp.

'They say one of the New York Mafia bosses was jealous of Bugsy. Also that Lansky and the others had decided in Cuba to do Bugsy in because he was holding out on them. With the six million they'd advanced him for the Flamingo! If Bugsy had stayed in one of the thirty-five rooms in his Holmby Hills mansion with his wife and kids . . . But he was in his mistress's house in Beverly Hills. Less than a hundred yards away, on Bedford, Johnny Stompanato was also killed. Another gangster, small fry. He was stabbed in Lana Turner's bedroom, by her teenage daughter! Out of jealousy or . . . maybe she was trying to protect her mother. No one knows. And right near there, on Rodeo, Lupe Velez, who was Gary Cooper's and Johnny Weismuller's sweetheart, killed herself. Not because of the cowboy or Tarzan—they'd divorced long before that. No, because some minor actor didn't want to marry her. Some nobody. She was pregnant. Took sleeping pills . . . like Marilyn.'

She fell silent for a moment. Maybe she realized she was going around in circles. That Marilyn's name and all the names and happenings of which she was speaking, as though they were timeless—for that was the undertone whenever June talked about the stars—were forcing her into a fateful circle, never letting her reach the center. June took a deep breath, as if to get a second wind.

'Well, anyway, Betty and I had a good time at the Flamingo. Did I mention that already? And then . . . then the day came for us to leave. We got up early. Studio people always get up earlier than most. We were all ready, had our bags packed, and were just leaving our room. I'm standing by a pane of glass on the third floor, looking out. In those days, you could see clear out into the desert—there were no tall buildings in the way. And suddenly, Lord help me, the pane shuddered, the floor shook, the walls wobbled, my suitcase fell over . . . My first thought was—an earthquake! and I shout, "It's an earthquake!" And then I see something and I move even closer to the window because I can't believe it. I see this enormous explosion way off in the distance . . . a huge cloud . . . not a mushroom, no, it spreads across the whole sky. As if they've blown up a whole town out there . . . Everyone's seen it, everyone. "What the hell is that?" people yell, and Betty turns to me and says,

"You know what, that's the bomb! They've just set off an atom bomb." Betty had read about it somewhere, about tests in Nevada. And suddenly everyone wanted to get out of there as fast as possible. I saw whole families racing to their cars and driving away like maniacs. And we, too, ran with our suitcases across the street, jumped on the bus, and told the driver to floor it. And the people on the bus . . . were all crying. We were the only ones who weren't crying. We sat there—maybe we were hard-hearted. The rest were crying and moaning, the fear was contagious, the fear that the thing that darkened the sky might blow in our direction once the wind changed. The driver went as fast as he could. We were all so innocent in those days. Naive! I mean, it would never have occurred to us that they'd do something like that, before our eyes, without warning. True, they'd told the press. But the press, those idiots, what did they do? They sent a bunch of young reporters with cameras. And they all got their story. Many of them died as a result. I personally know seven people who died because they got exposed that day.'

On the television screen—a commercial was on— Cal Worthington in a cowboy hat was walking along the endless row of used cars he was selling. One incredible deal after another. Cal took off his cowboy hat and invited us to stop by and see him that very day.

In the next shot, it seemed as though Genghis Khan had taken Cal up on his invitation. He rode up on his horse, dismounted and walked towards the car dealer in that unique gait of his, to take the 'cherry-red, hot '02 Mustang' Cal had been raving about for a test drive.

'And then, listen to this,' June continued, 'we're back in L.A. and I'm back at Fox and Betty at Disney. And, of course, we secretaries hear about everything that's going on, in the other studios, too. Now everyone was talking. When we set out on our little trip, no one suspected anything and now everyone knew. And we heard the stuff was already up in the stratosphere and then we heard it was going to blow towards L.A.. There was total panic. Where could we run to? Then we heard it was headed for San Francisco instead. The same panic broke out there. Then it was Reno. Everyone in this whole damned area was terrified. I mean, who'd given the go-ahead for those tests? What were they thinking? That Nevada's on the moon? Cut off from the rest of the country? And then, one or two years later, these boys come along . . .' June pointed briefly at the television screen (I noticed that like John Wayne she always indicated the direction with a slightly wavy motion) '. . . and shoot *The Conqueror* there. In the Escalante Valley in Utah, a hundred and fifty miles away, where the stuff came down. In Snow

Canyon there was a fine layer of gray ash on the sand. And that's where they shot dozens of battle scenes. For days, they had hundreds of riders galloping up and down the canyon. And then they come back to L.A. And I heard from other secretaries that they wanted to do a few pick-up shots on the MGM lot— you know, the night scenes by the campfire, scenes in and around Genghis Khan's tent, when those Mongols are singing and dancing, that kind of thing. And what do those idiots do? For the sake of consistency, they want the sand in the studio to have exactly the same reddish color as in the scenes shot on location, so they send a caravan of trucks up to Snow Canyon. They load them up with that shit and bring it back to MGM, where they dump it right in the middle of the studio. And then they have a whole crew of workmen with rakes and shovels turn it into a first-class desert. I assume they shot all kinds of scenes in that mess of ash. At any rate . . . someone got nervous. A great hue and cry. "We need a Geiger counter," they were saying. When they hold the thing over the sand, it starts crackling and buzzing. At that point they knew what they were up against. Except that no one knew how to get rid of the stuff. So they loaded it into the trucks again and had them haul it back to Snow Canyon, where they dumped it. Later I heard they'd burned the ground and the flooring where the stuff was put down at MGM. I suppose that helped.'

June cast one last look at the screen which was showing a scene from the twelfth century somewhere in the Utah Gobi. Hayward was dancing in front of Wayne and the assembled cast. June switched off the TV.

'Well, "helped" is relative. Of the two hundred people who worked on that film, almost half later died of cancer.'

Upstairs, I could see light in Pete's apartment and, through the blinds, the flickering of TV images was visible. Why had he not come down to join us? He had been the first one to tell me about June's birthday.

June and Jennifer had spent some time describing Jennifer's job, the sequences she had sketched thus far for the New Regency project. They also mentioned a young director who had a three-picture deal with Paramount and, as Jennifer had just discovered, had his heart set on working with her.

'Yes, Jennifer's being talked up,' June commented, not without pride. 'Word's getting around, and they like your ideas, your . . . Even at the studios, they're talking about you. Be careful is all I can say! Watch your back. When I was a secretary and they loaned me out—which happened all the time—I'd get to the new office and, as soon as the producer invited me in, I'd be sure to look at the couch. His couch. High heels leave little scratches. Or I'd pay close attention as we were talking. Quite a few of us fell into the trap. Your new boss would ask, "Are you married?" My friend Annabel said, "Separated. My husband and I live apart." "Hmmm. Do you have kids?" "Yes, a little girl," Annabel said, not suspecting a thing. And then he had her, the bastard. Told her straight out, "If you won't go to bed with me, you can say goodbye to your daughter." If she wasn't compliant, he'd make sure the authorities found out about the "loose woman" who was working in his office. And so on. Blackmail, plain and simple.'

'I'm telling you, the things I witnessed,' June said, 'those days were something else,' and it sounded as though she was looking for pretexts to take us back to those times. To the woman she once was.

'Once—pay attention to this, Jennifer; a person doesn't always have the presence of mind to realize what's happening—Jean Bello came to the office— that was Jean Harlow's mother—and wanted to give me a gift, a pair of golf gloves. Harlow had died quite a while ago and I suppose her mother found the gloves somewhere. Who knows what made her think of me. At any rate, she said, "Here, June, these are for you. They're Jean's golf gloves." And fool that I am, I try them on. In her presence! She's standing there and has just handed them to me across the desk. A present. Something—valuable! I can tell right away they're too small for me. Jean Harlow had very small hands. And believe it or not, I say, "No, ma'am, you should keep these." Those gloves would be worth a fortune today. What am I saying?—They already were then. A fortune!'

She poured herself, Jennifer and me a bit more champagne and I asked her, rather formally, whether that was a tradition in her family.

'What, to turn down presents, or . . . drink so much champagne?'

She laughed. We all laughed.

'No, I meant working for the studios,' I explained. 'Were your parents already . . .?'

'Oh, no,' she interrupted me. 'Not at all. We lived in Chicago, after all. I was the only one who wanted to get out of there. I was eighteen and ever since I'd seen Snow White, I'd been dreaming of working for Disney some day. At the time I had a job in Chicago, in the Wrigley Building on Lake Michigan. One day,

I fell in love at first sight—and unhappily—with a naval officer who strolled into our office chewing spearmint gum. I had this feeling, and sure enough, he promptly got a job with us. We saw each other every day after that and often went dancing. It didn't take long for me to realize he was seeing other women, too. Soon I couldn't take it any more. I decided I had to get away. So I moved to California, where I had relatives who ran a turkey ranch in Glendale. Where today the 5 crosses the 101, right near Disney Studios. The ranch is long gone, of course. And I got a job with Disney as a stenographer. The first thing they told me was, "Don't say 'Mr. Disney' to him when he comes in." "To him?" I asked, "When he comes in?" I couldn't believe that . . . that the Lord God would descend to earth to check on his typist. "Whatever you do, don't say 'Mr. Disney,'" they warned me, "he doesn't like that." Everyone was supposed to call him Walt, I heard. Simply Walt.

'And that afternoon he comes in, Mr. Disney does, says hello to everyone and—he already knows my name. My mouth went dry. I couldn't say a word. He already knew about me. "Hi, June," Disney says. I can't even manage to say, "Hi, Walt." Was I ever relieved when he disappeared into the next room. But God came and went, there was no avoiding him: "Hi, June!" And at some point—he must have noticed what a hard time I was having—he stopped and waited, smiling at me. "Hi . . ." I said. And blushed. "Yes?" he said, still waiting. "Hi, Walt," I said, red as a beet. Disney was enjoying himself. "OK," he said, "no more apples for Snow White here," and the others all laughed. I joined in, as best I could.

'No, that was the most important decision I ever made in my life. To leave Chicago and go to Hollywood and work for the studios. But I shouldn't have got married. That was my big mistake. You hear that, Jennifer? Well, I'm sure you know already.'

'I didn't know you were married, June,' I said.

'Well, I was, for fourteen years, let's not exaggerate. But that was the next mistake. Fourteen years. It's a mystery to me how I stood it. A damned mystery.'

'And who was he?'

'An actor, what else? A young, good-looking fellow. His father was a producer with Fox. I worshipped him. A splendid man, my father-in-law. And he knew it. He said to me right away, "You're too good for him." Boyd. Boyd Tarkington was the son's name. That was the name he went by professionally. Altogether he married eight times. I was number four. He never said a thing about the ones before me. A year or two was all they could take. Number three

167

crashed her private plane over the Grand Canyon. That's how she escaped after half a year of marriage. Then it was my turn. I advised him to give up acting, because it was so uncertain. He was getting hardly any parts. He managed to get hired as a cutter's assistant. He liked it, too. At least that's what he said. Later, he wanted to work with Elmo, who was with Disney at the time, and he did serve as his assistant for a while. But there were always problems with him. He never did make it to cutter. And Elmo was the best in the business. He was the cutter for *High Noon*, which brought him an Oscar. He saved that movie, many people say. But Boyd drove me completely crazy with his . . . with all his women. He couldn't keep his pants zipped!

'One time . . . that was really the worst, when I was most vulnerable. I'd gotten a job with Columbia Pictures. The first day. The entrance to the studios was on Gower, quite far south of Sunset. When you came into the lobby, the elevator was right there on your left. The elevator I had to take. To the office on the third floor. On the fourth, I knew, Harry Cohn had his suite, Columbia's boss. When I get on the elevator—someone's already in there. He stays on. Doesn't get off. Waits. Waits to see what I'm going to do. There's no one else in the elevator. Harry Cohn was famous for his womanizing. He was standing behind me in the elevator. Staring at me. It felt like an X-ray. Went straight through me. I'm not going to be able to stand this all the way to the third floor, I thought. But when the doors opened I stood there as if paralyzed. Finally I managed to take one step, but every bone in my body hurt.

'One day I was told they needed a good stenographer in a projection room. My assignment was to keep an eye on the screen and describe what I saw, shot by shot. "Be sure not to miss anything," I was told. Nothing out of the ordinary, I thought. Cramped shoulders for a week or two. The projector would be running from eight in the morning till six at night, with an hour's break for lunch. It turned out to be probably the worst week in my life.

'When I got to the projection room, they'd already turned off the lights. I saw a couple of people sitting in the first two or three rows, people I didn't recognize. Screenwriters, I thought. Of course I didn't ask. I hurried to my seat in the last row, because the show had begun. I located the small desk with a lamp, which I switched on. Then I opened the first steno pad I'd brought with me. You keep the little finger on your right hand stiff'—June demonstrated for us—'so you don't lose your place while you're taking steno and watching the screen at the same time.

'I see that all the scenes are silent. Not a sound in the room. The couple of people I noticed down below as I came in aren't talking. I see thirty-foot logs . . . make a note of that . . . that are first laid next to each other, then on top of each other. Then they dump some liquid on them. I have to record what I'm seeing but, at the same time, I'm thinking: Is that water being poured on them? What should I write?

'Suddenly the whole thing goes up in flames. I write, without letting the screen out of my sight: "Doused with gasoline." Then I see—and write down: "Movement in the middle of the fire." I note: "Looks as though someone is moving." Continue writing—and I'm thinking, June, you're nuts, they're going to fire you, you're hallucinating—and I write: "People moving as if trying to escape."

'My little finger is drilling into the paper—I can't do this. But I have to write, have to keep writing: "Full of people. The fire full of people. Dead, presumably. But I think some of them are still alive." I record it all. For three days. Three days, from eight to six, I describe every image that's projected. All those silent German, American and Russian images from the concentration camps. I had to find words for them. "Long scene. Looks as though they're digging up a meadow," I write. And then it was . . . I don't recall whether it was Americans or Russians doing the

170

digging . . . at any rate, they found a mass grave. Massacred corpses. And I had to write it down. I don't know what they needed it for. They were preparing some screenplay, I guess. Writing, writing . . .

'When I went home that first night, taking the bus—we lived on Hayworth, in the Fairfax district—Boyd was home, and I felt so sick and must have looked so wretched that of course he asked what was wrong. So I began to tell him. But he interrupted me immediately, saying he didn't want to hear about it. He wasn't in the mood, he was preparing for a part, had an audition to go to, that very evening, in fact, what do I know. When I kept on talking, more or less to myself, feeling utterly miserable, he shouted at me that I was tactless to bring stuff like that home with me. No sooner was he out of the house than his father called. Sam said it was urgent that he speak with me, that very evening if possible. "Of course," I said, "come on by." "Not at your place," he said. So I met him an hour later at Schwab's. He was already there when I arrived. He hemmed and hawed, spoke in a whisper . . . I figured it had to be something bad and I wouldn't be able to share my problems with him, which I'd secretly been hoping I could. "It's about your husband," he said suddenly. Yesterday he'd come to see them—his parents, that is. Nothing unusual about that, I thought. "He had a colleague with him, as he called her." "A colleague," I said, "what of it?" And Sam said, "Believe me, I'm familiar with that kind of colleague. I could tell right away that something was going on between them. Some starlet," Sam said, who went on and on about a part in *All about Eve*. "A Miss Monroe." So it was Marilyn Monroe with whom Boyd was cheating on me. I'd seen the film a couple of weeks earlier. At the time she was a complete unknown. God knows that was no comfort to me.'

'Did you confront him?' Jennifer asked.

'Yes, but he just yelled at me and acted offended, claimed they were just "rehearsing" together.'

'That night I had the most terrible nightmares. And the next day I had to sit through even worse images. Had to write it all down, every bit. The crazy part was that something inside me was trying to escape from those images even while I was obediently recording them. I tried to focus on something else. That something was jealousy, which I wouldn't have given in to otherwise. Boyd and that blond bitch. So the images and the horror they filled me with blended with jealous fantasies, the filthy stuff happening between him and her. It was sheer madness.

'After three days, I'd filled fourteen steno pads. Which then had to be transcribed, of course. That would take another three days. The two Polish girls who shared my office at Columbia took pity on me. They saw that I was at the end of my rope. One of them offered to help me with the typing. She said I could dictate to her. But I lied, saying that wouldn't work because her knowledge of English spelling was still shaky, and there couldn't be any mistakes. She looked at me as though I'd rejected her friendship. The two Polish girls had numbers tattooed on their forearms. Now I knew, or at least sensed what that meant. All I'd done was spend three days in a projection room, whereas those girls . . . God, it's impossible to imagine. Words are nothing compared to what they'd experienced! All I'd done was eavesdrop, so to speak. Nonetheless, every night I locked the transcribed pages in the file cabinet. Less because I was afraid the girls might see them than . . . I was afraid for myself. Afraid of being dragged in deeper, of drowning in their terrible wounds. Who can wear the star? I'd been initiated and the burden others had to bear was crushing me. On Saturday morning, I was finally done.

'I remember I left the office and went down the corridor, the long corridor to the elevator. And who's coming towards me? Gene Kelly, I kid you not, Gene Kelly. My big crush. I've no idea what brought him there. Maybe he'd gotten off on the wrong floor.

Suddenly—this was completely crazy—I was overcome by a tearing desire . . . to dance with him! Actually I'm a dancer, or rather, I always wanted to be one. At any rate, I wanted to dance with him, at that very moment, and I go up to him, determined to say, "Come, Gene, let's dance!"

'And I would have sung something, too, it didn't matter what, just to get to dance with him. Gene Kelly moves like no one else, he has perfect control of his body . . .'

June clapped her hands as though she could see him dancing, clapped in time to every move.

' . . . and he wants to, I can tell, wants me to dance with him, and I . . .'—she clapped again—'I didn't do it.

'I walked right by him. Stiff as a board. And I said to myself, "You coward, you're nothing but a coward. You don't even know how to make sure you have something worth remembering. What kind of memories do you want to have stored up when you're old and gray?"

'Sometimes I still have those . . . nightmares. I step into a projection room. It's dark. And it stays dark and silent. And the silence and the darkness drain away my courage, to the point that I can't take another step. In life.

'I never could tell my father about those films. Couldn't have brought myself to. He'd have . . . it would've killed him, I think.

'My father was a Jew. A German Jew. His name was Samuel, Sam . . . like my father-in-law. Sam's father, my grandfather, came here from Germany with his wife and child and tried to find work in New York as a photographer. That didn't work out, so they moved to Milwaukee. There my grandfather abandoned the family. For another woman. Just up and left. At the age of six, my father stood on the street corner selling newspapers to keep the family afloat. Later he was taken in by an uncle, I think. Then my grandmother remarried. Andrew Barker, who adopted my father. He was twelve when he became Sam Barker, so he understood perfectly what was going on.

'On my fifteenth birthday . . . good Lord, that was sixty-two years ago, my father had me blow out the candles, and then made all of us pile into the car—my younger sister, my mother and the birthday child in the back, behind him. 'We're going for a drive,' he said. While he was driving, he had me rub his neck and shoulders now and then. It turned into a long drive. We drove from Chicago to Milwaukee. Drove all day and then drove around Milwaukee.

'At one point, he stopped the car and put on the emergency brake. We were in a residential neighborhood, in front of a house. And we simply sat there. A couple of times it looked as if he were going to get out. Without us. I thought, they had a fight. The night before my birthday I'd heard their voices, so loud they'd woken me up, and now, I thought, he's going to leave us. Get out and leave us in the car. My mother, sitting in front, looked crushed. I think she was crying, trying to hide it from us. Finally I say, "Dad, what's wrong? Why are we stopping here?" And he replied, "You're old enough now. It's time for you to be told." Without looking, he pointed at the house. "That's where my father lives. My real father. He left us when I was six. I hardly remember him. They told me he's dying." He'd heard it from his cousins. They were like brothers and sometimes when they came to visit, they'd go down to the basement for man-to-man talks. "Dying," he said, "he's dying and I should probably go inside to pay my respects . . . But I just can't make myself. I don't know the man."

'Then he started the car and we drove away. We children didn't care one way or the other, you know. After all, the man meant nothing to us. I never saw him, not even a picture.

'And now you're here,' June said to Jennifer. 'You close the loop for me. You had no way of knowing that.'

'I'm sure he has no idea what you're talking about,' Jennifer responded, and turned to me: 'My mother died a few years ago. Among her things, I found a package meant for June. There was a note to that effect attached to it and I kept meaning to get the package to her. And then yesterday, I finally . . .'

'Why didn't you and your mother ever visit me?' June interrupted.

'I don't know,' Jessica replied. 'Something always came up. I thought the two of you had had a falling out. She mentioned some such thing. There were a couple of times when you came out to Pasadena to visit us, when I was a child.'

'It doesn't matter,' June said. 'It doesn't matter what happened. Now you're here and you've even stayed an extra day to celebrate my birthday with me. You don't know what that means to me. I always thought, "I'm the last one." And that's been true, ever since my younger sister died. But now that I've seen you, it feels different.'

'Really?'

'Really, it feels different. As if . . . as if we had a bit of a future.'

We saw that June was holding back tears. To distract us, she began digging around in the pocket of her blue terrycloth bathrobe. Without looking Jennifer in the eye, she handed her a bunch of keys.

'Here . . . go get the package you brought me. In a few minutes we're going to have a toast.'

June looked at her watch and thus did not see that Jennifer hesitated but then got up and walked along the pool to the stairs leading to the second floor.

'What was your father's name again, June?' I asked her.

'My father? Sam Barker,' she said absentmindedly.

'I mean his German name,' I said.

'I didn't mention it, babe,' June said, her voice suddenly bitter. And then, somewhat more softly, as if she were trying to compose herself, 'I'm not telling. Oh, no. That's something I intend to keep to myself.'

She looked straight at me, as if suddenly another person were sitting there—as if she were confused to see that it was only me. She reached for her glass and pushed it away from her, her fingers trembling.

'But . . . but I'll tell you another name. Boyd. Boyd Tarkington. That was his stage name. His real name—but don't tell anyone, OK? You know him very well, I'm sure . . .'

At that moment we heard Jennifer calling from the landing outside June's apartment.

'I can't get the door open,' she called. 'Which key should I ...'

June remarked that Jennifer needed to pull the door towards her, there was nothing wrong with the key. She asked me to go up and help, and to bring down the bottle of champagne I would see in the refrigerator.

'And bring a proper champagne glass for yourself,' she called after me, 'and a candle.'

I helped Jennifer open the door, realizing only after it opened that, with the exception of a few glimpses through the cracked door when I was on my way to Pete's, I had never seen the inside of June's apartment.

The air conditioner was turned up high. The only light on was in the kitchen. Draped over the back of the armchair was Rex's blue towel. I recognized the faded stars.

Jennifer squeezed past me in the semi-darkness, reached quickly for an opened cardboard box—an old shoebox, I thought—and pushed away the grease-spotted brown wrapping paper and the cut twine. She did not head downstairs immediately but came into the kitchen, as if she wanted to prevent me from poking around in June's apartment.

'Are you finding what you need?'

'Yes, I've got it,' I said, closed the refrigerator and picked up a sparkling-clean wine glass standing next to the sink.

'No, take one of the champagne glasses,' she said, and reached up into a cabinet next to the stove. 'She told you to, after all.'

'Have you looked at those?' I pointed to the wall above June's couch, piled high with pillows.

On the wall, along with an old peacock feather full of eyes, hung three framed pictures. They looked to me like original animation cells from Disney films. Only one of them could be identified at a glance. It hung close to the door, where some light fell on it from the fixture on the balcony.

'That's from *Snow White*,' Jennifer said. '"Walt" supposedly signed it for her when she left.'

It was one of the cells showing Snow White in the coffin, when the creatures of the forest come and lay flowers around the glass bier.

'Come on already,' Jennifer called.

On the stroke of midnight, we drank to June's birthday. She had put on bright-red lipstick, the wind had blown out the candle and June had lit it again. The air was cooler now.

'It's lovely to have a visit from my relative,' June said. She stood up as though about to make a speech to Jennifer.

'Who knows how much longer we have,' she remarked, 'before the broom sweeps clean. Hmm. But one thing . . . I can say. And for that I have you to thank, Jennifer dear. The secret that was withheld from me, the touch my father wasn't capable of, because at the time he lacked the strength . . .'

She broke off, sat down, took a deep breath. Then she reached for the shoebox and opened it.

As she lifted out the square tin canister, she continued, 'Now, I'm thinking, I can help us, both of us. I have the means here in my hands, see?'

She sat there, full of emotion, not saying a word. Finally she leaned forward as if trying to decipher an inscription. But then she stood up resolutely. Moving quickly to the side of the pool, she took the cover off the canister and shook its contents into the water.

It was her grandfather's ashes, the ashes of the man she had never seen, which trickled into the illuminated pool. The canister's cover fell from her hand, sliced through the bright water and, tumbling and floating, followed the ashes. Like a chalice that invisible hands passed wildly back and forth. To gather up here and there some of what was spilled.

None of us spoke. We watched the ashes, which, as they fell, guided by tiny currents, fanned out and began to take on shapes. When I restricted myself to watching the threads of ash—for some of the particles stuck together—I was reminded of my dream, saw the horse's head, as if it were forming here anew, as if the same image were finding a voice here.

The lid settled silently to the bottom of the pool and you could see that the heaviest particles and clumps had already joined it while others, the lightest ones, had hardly descended below the surface. I saw that a figure had coalesced in the water, floating deep and broad, a cloud in the likeness of a man.

Jennifer saw it, too, I was certain. She was standing only two feet away.

Without our having noticed her—she must have darted behind our backs—June was suddenly standing at the other end of the pool . . . and dove in, parting the water with her head.

Up above, on the edge of the balcony—I noticed him only because I had stepped back a few feet—stood Pete, gazing down at us.

With three or four powerful kicks June reached the bottom and groped along, more slowly now, through the sparkling threads of ash as they drifted apart. She dove upward, as if under the billowing hem of a bridal gown, into the midst of the drifting figure, into the center of the light-pierced dancing cloud.

At the bottom of the pool rested the latch to the canister.

She reached for it and, kneeling, looked up towards the surface. Slowly she stood erect in the water. The daughter of man.

At that moment I felt as if I were standing down there with her and saw myself surrounded by the universe, swaddled in wholeness, waiting, standing, floating in the ancestral dust. Disporting myself inside, as yet unconceived. It felt as though my hand, along with hers, were now drawn upward, slowly pointing to something—a swirling island of dust, a kernel of ash within it. Now it was fixed by the eye. It felt as though I knew, along with her, whence it came, where it had once glowed, when it was still fire in the body.

At that, June crouched once more and pushed off powerfully from the bottom of the pool, thrust through the dust to the crown, the cloud's head, and rose out of the water.

She swam quickly, with strong strokes, to the lip of the pool, pulled herself out of the water without hesitation, as if it held no memories, as if she were carrying everything upward within herself, born anew.